Roarke had only heard that voice once, but he'd never forget it.

Roarke scanned the woman. She was gorgeous in a floor-length blue gown that reminded him of something a Greek goddess would wear. The smooth, creamy skin of her back and shoulders gleamed, highlighted with a dusting of glitter that augmented her ethereal beauty.

Roarke glanced at her left hand. The huge rock she'd been sporting a few nights earlier was notably absent.

One corner of Annabel's mouth curled in a grin as she took another sip of her martini. She leaned in and whispered, "I don't know if you know this, but you're staring. It's frowned upon in polite society."

Before he could respond, she pressed a hand to his chest, lifted onto her toes and planted a soft kiss on his lips.

Roarke froze, startled.

Annabel laughed. "I can't figure out if the kiss was that bad or that good."

"It was good. Definitely...good."

* * *

Off Limits Lovers is part of the Texas Cattleman's Club: Houston series.

Dear Reader,

Both love and hate prompt people to take extraordinary actions. Nowhere is that more apparent than in the realm of wealthy rivals Sterling Perry and Ryder Currin with its maze of family secrets, shocking scandals and unexpected love affairs. In the Texas Cattleman's Club: Houston series we discover what happens when someone is brave enough to pull back the curtain of blind hatred and search for the truth.

In *Off Limits Lovers,* jaded attorney Roarke Perry falls for free-spirited entrepreneur Annabel Currin— a jilted bride who hires him to recoup monetary losses from her ex-fiancé. Meanwhile, a scandalous rumor threatens to derail the budding relationship between Ryder Currin and Angela Perry.

Thank you for joining me for this installment of Texas Cattleman's Club: Houston. For more outrageous fun, be sure to read the complete series.

To discover my Bourbon Brothers and Pleasure Cove series, visit reeseryan.com/desirereaders. For series news, reader giveaways and more, join my VIP Readers newsletter list.

Until our next adventure,

Reese Ryan

REESE RYAN

———

OFF LIMITS LOVERS

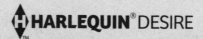
HARLEQUIN® DESIRE

Special thanks and acknowledgment are given to Reese Ryan for her contribution to the Texas Cattleman's Club: Houston miniseries.

ISBN-13: 978-1-335-60380-7

Off Limits Lovers

Recycling programs for this product may not exist in your area.

HARLEQUIN®
www.Harlequin.com

Printed in U.S.A.

Reese Ryan writes sexy, emotional love stories served with a side of family drama. The 2017 *Los Angeles Times* Festival of Books panelist and 2018 Donna Hill Breakout Author Award recipient is the author of the Bourbon Brothers and Pleasure Cove series. Connect with Reese via Instagram, Facebook and Twitter, or on reeseryan.com. Join her VIP Readers Lounge at bit.ly/VIPReadersLounge.

Books by Reese Ryan

Harlequin Desire

The Bourbon Brothers

Savannah's Secret
The Billionaire's Legacy
Engaging the Enemy

Dynasties: Secrets of the A-List

Seduced by Second Chances

Texas Cattleman's Club: Houston

Off Limits Lovers

You can find Reese Ryan on Facebook, along with other Harlequin Desire authors, at Facebook.com/harlequindesireauthors!

To all of the amazing readers who read and recommend my books. I'm so grateful you've chosen to come along for the ride.

To my fellow author and accountability buddy, Amalie Berlin, thank you for your support and selfless generosity.

One

Annabel Currin held up a cocktail dress in the mirror at one of her favorite boutiques. The backless light blue goddess gown with a high side slit had a very classic feel. Yet, it also had a bit of the Bohemian vibe that was part of her signature style. She needed to get her mind off the terrible fight she'd had with her fiancé, Mason Harrison, and its ugly aftermath, which still had her reeling.

But she didn't want to think about any of that today.

"What do you think?" Annabel stared at her friend Frankie Walsh's reflection in the mirror.

A broad smile spread across the woman's face and her green eyes twinkled. "I love that color against your complexion, Annabel. You're going to look amazing in that dress at the American Cancer Society gala. Wait until Mason sees you in this."

"You think so?" Annabel scrunched her nose as she studied her honey-colored skin. The product of a father with deep Irish roots and a Kenyan mother with gorgeous, deep brown skin. Her question was in reference to the earlier part of her friend's statement. She couldn't care less what Mason would think about the dress.

"Absolutely. You look incredible in everything. You could wear an oversize T-shirt to this event and half the internet would be trying to copy you."

"Thanks." Annabel gave the woman a warm smile, glad she and Frankie had become friends.

She'd given Francesca Walsh, a hand on the Currin Ranch at the time, an impromptu makeover for a big event she was attending that night with Annabel's older brother, Xander. A lot had changed in the short time since then. Frankie was now Xander's fiancée and the newly discovered long-lost heir to the Langley fortune.

The casual acquaintance they'd formed during that makeover had grown into a bona fide friendship after Xander and Frankie's engagement. She was a bubbly, incredibly sweet person. Annabel's brother was lucky to have her.

Frankie bit her lower lip and frowned.

"What is it?" Annabel asked.

"Our friendship is still new, so tell me if I'm crossing any boundaries here." Frankie sucked in a deep breath. "But is something going on with you today?"

"Why do you ask?" Annabel turned back to the mirror for one last look at the dress. Then she hung it on a rack with a few others they'd selected as contenders.

"You don't seem like your usual confident self. Yesterday, you were giddy. You said you had this big happy secret you couldn't wait to tell us all about. And today you're like… I don't know." Frankie tugged her hair, twisted into a single long braid, over one shoulder. "A deflated balloon. Like you're just going through the motions. I get the distinct impression it's related to that disagreement you had with Mason. The one you don't want to talk about. Is everything okay between you two?"

Annabel's eyes stung with tears. She didn't respond. She focused on her work instead—the real reason they were there. To capture footage for her popular vlog channel.

She was a fashion vlogger with a huge following, and the boutique owner, who was sponsoring this episode, was comping her a dress for a charity gala she'd be attending.

Annabel often gifted makeovers to followers locally or when she attended fashion and makeup industry events. But she'd decided to go beyond playing fairy godmother to a few select women. She'd decided to open Fairy Godmother, a local consignment shop and a salon that offered makeover services, which would allow her to help a lot more people.

She ignored her friend's question as she busied herself with setting up the camera lighting. "Now that I have a handful of options, I'll record the vlog post 'discovering' each of the dresses. I'll discuss why they work for my body type and complexion. I'll also show a few of the dresses that didn't work for me, including an honest assessment of why they didn't. Then I'll try on all of the final contenders before selecting 'the one.'"

"Did I overstep?" Frankie had asked to come along and help. She stooped to take the next lighting fixture out of its storage case to set it up.

"No, of course not. You're just a little too good at this friendship thing, I guess." Annabel gave a nervous laugh. She studied Frankie for a moment, then cleared her throat. "Hey, if I told you something, could you keep it just between us for now? Even from my brother?"

Frankie seemed to roll the request over in her head. "It's nothing dangerous or life-threatening, right? Nothing he needs to know?"

"No, nothing like that."

A slow smile lit Frankie's green eyes. She squeezed Annabel's arm. "Then, of course."

"Actually, maybe it would be better if I showed you after we're done here." Annabel sighed, hoping that this reveal would go better than the last.

Butterflies flitted in Annabel's stomach as she opened the rusty lock and led Frankie through the doors of a small older building that had once been a celebrated hair salon.

Her favorite pair of old, worn black-and-brown

cowboy boots clopped against the tile floor as they walked inside. The stale air and lingering pungent scent of leftover chemicals assaulted their senses. Dust swirled in the sunlight peeking through the dirty front windows.

"We're standing in the heart of what will become Fairy Godmother." Annabel ran her fingers through her hair, fashioned in microbraids. The hair nearest her scalp was braided, while the majority of its length fell in loose waves down her back. "I purchased the connected building next door, too. That's where the vintage clothing store will be. But clients can get complete makeovers here. I'm talking hair, skin, makeup and nails. All available as a paid service, which will allow me to do more Fairy Godmother makeovers for deserving women trying to reenter the workplace."

"What a fantastic idea, Annabel." Frankie beamed. "And this place is incredible. I adore lovely old buildings like this. When was it built?"

"It was completed in 1934. Thus the art deco style." Annabel indicated the geometric wallpaper design and the beautiful terrazzo flooring with its intricate geometric pattern.

"This place will be absolutely stunning once you've renovated it. Then maybe accent it with some vintage pieces that would go well with the era of the architecture," Frankie went on excitedly.

Her friend had barely been able to tame her enthusiasm from the moment they walked through the door. Frankie's reaction was the exact opposite of

Mason's when she'd shown the old building to him and revealed her plans for it.

"That's what I was thinking, too." Annabel pointed to the space up front. "I'd love to get some comfy banquette seating built beneath the window and then along that wall."

After they explored the shop, Annabel showed her friend the building next door and shared her plans for it before the late-summer sun went down.

Frankie hugged her. "I'm so happy for you, Annabel. This was your dream and you're making it happen. What did Mason say?"

The joy and excitement Annabel had felt as she shared her plans with Frankie quickly faded. Mason's scowl and utter disappointment filled her brain. A ball tightened in her stomach.

Mason Harrison worked for her father. He was an executive at Currin Oil, where he'd been quickly ascending the corporate ladder. They'd been engaged for nearly a year and their wedding date was only a couple months away. But he'd been angry and dismissive when she told him of her plans.

"I brought him here after we had lunch together the other day. He accused me of behaving like an impetuous little girl by buying this place without consulting him or my father."

"I'm sure he was just surprised." Frankie tried to sound reassuring. "He'll come around."

"No. He won't," Annabel admitted, her throat tightening. "He wants me to settle down and be a 'proper' society wife. And he expects me to give up my 'little blog' once we're married."

"*Little* blog? You have hundreds of thousands of followers and dozens of top tier sponsors." Frankie folded her arms, indignant on her behalf. "You love what you do, and you're making a really good living at it. Why would Mason expect you to give it up?"

"He doesn't consider what I do a career, and he doesn't want his wife working in some 'run-down shack.' Evidently, being an entrepreneur isn't suitable for a 'proper society wife.'" She used air quotes again. "Mason gave me an ultimatum. I wouldn't budge." Annabel shrugged. "So he broke off our engagement."

"I'm sorry, Annabel. I didn't realize how serious the argument was." Frankie squeezed her arm. "Maybe Mason just needs to get used to the idea. And you're still wearing his ring, so I bet you two will resolve this before the gala this weekend."

"No." Annabel's unyielding tone seemed to surprise her friend. "Mason is looking for a trophy wife who'll be content hosting cocktail parties and attending charity functions just to make *him* look good. I feel incredibly stupid that I didn't recognize that before now." She twisted the ring on her finger, suddenly self-conscious about it.

Why was she still wearing Mason's engagement ring when it was clearly over between them?

Maybe some small part of her held out hope that they'd reconcile. But in talking to her friend, she realized something she hadn't wanted to admit before. Mason Harrison wasn't the man for her. She'd take the ring off once she'd told her father that the engagement was over. But she just hadn't been ready to do that.

"My father says he won't be able to attend the gala. Currin Oil is a platinum sponsor, so I need to be there to represent our family and the company." Annabel sighed. "Besides, this event is important to me. We lost my mom to cancer, so I'll do whatever I can to support this cause."

"I wish Xander and I didn't have plans that night. I hate to think of you there all alone." Frankie frowned.

"I'll be fine. Promise." Annabel forced a smile for the sake of her friend.

"Usually, I'd offer a platitude like time heals all wounds, but I don't think that's what you want to hear right now." Frankie wrapped an arm around her shoulder. "So let's focus on the fact that you've taken the first step to fulfilling your dream. That calls for a celebration. And pie."

Annabel grinned. "You had me at pie."

Two

Roarke Perry exited his rental SUV and stepped inside Farrah's Coffee Shop. He smiled fondly as he inhaled the familiar scent. Dark, rich Columbian-roast
coffee and a wide range of delicious pies. He'd always
loved this little place. They had amazing coffee and
Ms. Farrah made the best Texas pecan fudge pie in the
state. Before he saw his father, Sterling Perry, again
for the first time in years he needed both.

He got in line behind two women; one of them
was a very pretty tomboy with a long brown braid
over one shoulder. The other was a gorgeous biracial
woman with high cheekbones, dark almond-shaped
eyes and miles of smooth creamy skin. She wore cutoff jean shorts, a flouncy off-the-shoulder Bohemian
blouse and her long legs were capped by a pair of

broken-in brown-and-black cowboy boots. Her dark hair fell down her back in waves.

There was something about her voice and the sound of her laugh that captivated him.

The woman ordered a slice of lemon icebox pie and her friend ordered cherry. When she turned to leave, she nearly collided with him, but he reached out and grabbed her shoulders, halting her.

"Oh, my gosh, I'm so sorry. I wasn't paying attention to where I was going."

"No worries. The important thing is we saved the pie." He winked at her.

Her dark eyes twinkled as they studied his.

Something about her almost seemed familiar. The way she stared at him made him wonder if she didn't feel the same. But he wasn't about to trot out that old, tired line. Especially since the woman was sporting a sizable engagement ring on her slim finger.

It was just as well. His reasons for returning to Houston were anything but social. And in just a few days, he'd be returning to Dallas. His home since college.

"Well, thank you for saving my pie." She lifted the small dessert plate. "My apologies again."

He tipped an imaginary Stetson and nodded as she and her friend made their way to a booth near the back of the coffee shop.

The gorgeous woman's fiancé was a very lucky guy.

Roarke owned a luxury condominium in town in the same building where his older twin sisters, Angela and Melinda, owned condos. But the executive he'd leased it to wouldn't be vacating the space for a few more days. So he got into the SUV and headed toward Perry Ranch—his family's opulent, sprawling estate just outside Houston.

The Perry family's lifestyle was financed by Perry Holdings, a billion-dollar operation that consisted of finance, construction, real estate and property management entities.

Sterling Perry's name carried a lot of clout in Houston, a city where his father wielded much power. Though apparently not enough to prevent him from being accused of running a Ponzi scheme that caused clients to lose millions of dollars. Nor had it prevented him from being tossed into jail. Much to Sterling's surprise, to be sure.

Roarke was an attorney. Though, much to his father's chagrin, he'd chosen not to work for Perry Holdings. Instead, his Dallas-based civil law practice represented underserved clients who typically couldn't afford to pay a retainer up front. Still, from his office in Dallas, he'd taken an active role in helping to clear his father of the charges that had been leveled against him.

Sterling Perry had the ethics of a rattlesnake. It sickened Roarke that he'd spent countless hours trying to defend the man when he had clients whose cases required his full attention.

Most sons would defend their fathers against such accusations with their last breaths. Even if their fathers weren't bastions of decency, the familial bond made them *want* to believe the best of their fathers.

Roarke and Sterling Perry shared no such bond.

He was the youngest of the Roarke brood and Sterling's only son. But he was by no means the apple of his father's eye. A reality that had pained him throughout his childhood.

No matter what he did, or how hard he tried, his father never gushed with pride, the way he had over even the smallest accomplishments of his three older sisters. As a young boy, he'd been starved for his father's approval. As a teenager, he'd resolved himself to the fact that there was nothing he could do to earn the man's affections.

Roarke could believe a host of horrible things about Sterling Perry. That he was running a Ponzi scheme simply wasn't one of them.

His father had considered Bernie Madoff and his ilk delusional rubes for thinking they could pull off such a scheme. Besides, Perry Holdings Inc. was flush with cash. There was no earthly reason his father would've been enticed to take such a risk.

Those were the reasons he firmly believed in his father's innocence. Not because they shared a surname.

But even his father's arrest hadn't been reason enough for him to come home. He'd worked on the case and consulted with his father's lawyers from his office in Dallas.

He'd come home for one reason. At his sister Angela's request, he was here to prove, once and for all, he was *not* the son of Ryder Currin—the sworn enemy of their father and the man his sister had been seeing for the past several months.

Angela had called him in Dallas, panicked after she'd met with an old family friend. Lavinia Cardwell was a wealthy local philanthropist, a major contributor to the Texas Cattleman's Club, and a notorious gossip.

Lavinia had informed his sister about the rumor that he was really Ryder Currin's son. A rumor Roarke was well aware that his own father believed, though he'd never, ever mentioned it to any of them. His sister had asked Ryder to prove that it wasn't true by agreeing to a paternity test.

To Ryder's credit, he had.

Roarke didn't believe the rumors, but if it would save his sister's sanity and finally put those old rumors to bed, it would be worth it.

He pulled the SUV up to the guard post on his family's vast estate and greeted the older man who'd been the head security guard since Roarke was a teen.

"Good to see you, Mr. Perry." A slow smile spread across Ben Mattison's face as he reached out to shake his hand. "Your family is eagerly awaiting your arrival."

"You mean *my sisters* are eagerly awaiting my arrival." Roarke stared at the house, his jaw tense. When he looked back at Ben, there was a slight downturn of the man's mouth. An all too familiar look of pity dimmed his eyes.

"If you don't mind me saying, sir, I'm quite sure

the old man misses you, too." Ben forced a smile as he tipped his hat and pushed the button to open the gate.

Roarke acknowledged the man's words with a nod, but time and experience had taught him the folly of allowing himself to believe them.

He entered the slowly opening iron gate and drove toward the sprawling stone mansion that had always reminded him of a castle out of place amid the pastures and elegant barns. By the time he arrived at the house and parked in the drive, Roarke's three sisters were already assembled on the large porch.

"Baby brother!" Esme, six years his senior, squealed, hugging him as soon as he exited the vehicle.

"You realize I'm almost thirty, right?" he asked as he released her.

"You realize I'll be calling you that when you're seventy, right?" she shot back, her blue eyes sparkling.

"Roarke!" Melinda ruffled his hair, much darker blond than her own, and hugged him tight. She was one of the fraternal twins and eleven years his senior. "It's about time you came home for a visit."

"I know." Roarke hadn't realized how much he'd missed his sisters. Surrounded by the trio of willowy blondes who he knew loved him without question, the tired excuses he usually made for not coming home felt lame, even to him. "But I'm here now. And I came bearing gifts. Take a look in the back seat."

Esme squealed again and she and Melinda were

chattering about Farrah's pies as Angela approached him and hugged him tight.

"Thank you so much for coming, Roarke. This means a lot to all of us, including Dad." Angela's gaze dropped when he gave her an incredulous frown. "But especially to me."

Roarke gathered his bags, and Angela took the leather messenger bag from him as they headed toward the house trailing behind Esme and Melinda, each carrying a pie.

He draped an arm over Angela's shoulder and lowered his voice, so only she could hear him. "By tomorrow night, you'll have a definitive answer. Then everything should be fine between you and Ryder."

"I don't know." She glanced up at him. "You should've seen his face when I confronted him about the rumor."

"Was he angry?" Roarke regarded his sister with concern.

"Worse. He was genuinely hurt that I wouldn't just accept his assertion that you couldn't possibly be his son." Her blue eyes glistened with tears. "I think maybe you were right. It may be impossible for us to recover from this."

"Wasn't the paternity test Ryder's idea?"

She nodded, quickly wiping away tears. "He was determined to prove it isn't true. He insists that he and Mom were only good friends. That he would never have… That they didn't…"

Angela hadn't been able to finish the thought, and Roarke was glad. He didn't want to contemplate the possibility. Their mother had died in a car crash the year he'd graduated high school. Without her as a buffer between him and his father and with his sisters off on their own, his time with Sterling had been intolerable. They'd both said things they could never take back. And at the end of that awful summer, he hadn't been able to leave for college fast enough.

"I understand how unsettling this must be for both of you. Just focus on one objective at a time. First resolve this concern. Then you two can address any issues of trust it may have caused." He'd said it as if it were the simplest thing in the world, despite knowing otherwise.

Angela forced a smile and nodded. "I might need to impose on you for one more thing, Roarke. Ryder was supposed to be my date for the American Cancer Society gala this weekend. I have to be there to represent Perry Holdings. I can't let it seem as if we're cowering and hiding while this investigation is going on. As if we believe Dad has done something wrong."

Roarke sighed and nodded. He'd hoped to get in and out quickly, seeing as few people in this town as necessary. But he wouldn't leave Angela sullen and alone at what he knew to be one of her favorite society events. "If you and Ryder haven't patched things up by then, I'll be your plus-one."

"Thanks, little brother." She slipped an arm around him. "I'm glad you're home. And one more thing… You need to tell Dad that you're a big part of the reason he's at home on house arrest rather than sitting in a jail cell right now."

"I'm done trying to make Sterling accept me, Ang. We are what we are." Roarke set his bag against the wall in the foyer. "I'm here because you asked me to come. That's it. The work I've been doing on his behalf I've been doing for you, Melinda and Esme. And for the Perry legacy."

"I understand. But wouldn't it be better to take credit for what you've done than to listen to him complain for the next three days about how his only son doesn't give a damn about him?"

"He's not entirely wrong." Roarke massaged the tension in his neck that intensified with every step he took toward Sterling Perry.

Angela elbowed his side. "You don't mean that."

He opened his mouth to object, but his sister fixed him with a stare, her arms folded.

"You *don't* mean that," she repeated.

He sighed. "Fine. Where is the old man, anyway?"

"Right here," his father called from atop the stairs, his voice stern. "Not that you care a single solitary lick." Sterling Perry descended the stairs. "I footed the bill for that fancy law degree you insist on wasting on small potatoes clients. Yet, you didn't use a whiff of what you learned to come to my aid."

"Hello to you, too, *Sterling*." Roarke usually didn't call his father that to his face, but the man had managed to piss him off within ten seconds of his arrival.

The older man scowled at the use of his name. "What brings you here, boy?"

Roarke's hands instantly curled into fists at his sides. A natural reaction to being raised by an asshole father who everyone else seemed to think walked on water.

At least they had prior to his father being accused of running a Ponzi scheme. Then there was the body that had been found at the building site of the new Houston chapter of the Texas Cattleman's Club. A construction site run by Perry Holdings. The victim hadn't been identified as of yet, and his father hadn't been formally implicated in the murder. But Roarke feared it was only a matter of time before investigators tried to pin that on Sterling, too.

"He's here to see you, of course, Dad." Melinda kissed her father on the cheek. "Why else would he be here?" She smiled sweetly at Roarke, but her eyes pleaded with him to just go along.

He'd spent his entire damn life "just going along" with Sterling Perry's nonsense. First, at the behest of his late mother. Then at the bidding of his sisters. It was the reason he hadn't been able to get out of there fast enough. And it was the reason he hadn't moved back.

Roarke had come to the conclusion that Houston wasn't big enough for him and Sterling Perry. And that was just fine by him. Dallas was his home now.

"In fact, Roarke didn't want you to know it, but he was instrumental in getting you released on house arrest. He's been working tirelessly behind the scenes to get you exonerated," Angela added quickly, before he could object.

"That true, boy?" Sterling walked toward him.

Roarke shoved his hands in his pockets and nodded. "Yes, sir. It is."

"Hmm." Sterling sniffed, as if weighing the possibility that his "worthless" son had been the one to secure his release.

"Seems to me that if you were able to get me out on house arrest, if you'd pushed a little harder, I'd be completely exonerated." Sterling shrugged in response to his daughters' groans of disapproval at his signature lack of gratitude. "Well, I am innocent, and he's supposed to be a hotshot *champion for the underdog.* I've done nothing wrong. Yet, I'm being treated like a common criminal."

Their father stuck his foot out and lifted his pant leg, revealing his ankle monitor. "This thing itches like the dickens."

"For once, Dad, could you at least *try* not to be so awful to Roarke?" Esme folded her arms, her voice sharp as she narrowed her gaze at their father. "Despite his busy caseload, Roarke found a way to get you released from that hellhole. And he dropped everything to come here."

Sterling inhaled deeply, looking as if his youngest daughter's words had pained him. Finally, he stuck out a hand and offered it to Roarke.

"Thank you for getting me out of there."

He shook his father's hand. "You're welcome."

"Now that you're here, you'll be able to investigate further. Someone set me up and as soon as I find out who, there'll be hell to pay. I can't live like this." He indicated the ankle bracelet again. "Not to mention what it's doing to my name and the value of our business. You have got to get to the root of this. Find out who did this to me. To all of us."

His father had a stable of high-priced lawyers. So how in the hell had he suddenly been tasked with being the lead investigator responsible for clearing Sterling Perry's name?

"I brought my case file, and there are a few people I'd like to question. See if they can shed a little more light on how this all got started." Roarke indicated the messenger bag Angela was carrying.

"Good, let's step into the den and talk shop."

"Now?" Roarke hoped to get a moment to regroup before sitting down to discuss the case.

"Can't think of a better time." Sterling headed into the den.

Roarke groaned, taking the bag from his sister as he followed his father to the den. He hadn't been there five minutes and already Sterling was manipulating him. He couldn't get on that return flight to Dallas fast enough.

He took a seat and met his father's stare. "Do you have any ideas about who might've set you up?"

"You're damn right I do." His father flicked a glance toward the entry hall, where his sisters were chattering about putting the pies on plates. Sterling closed the door, then sat in a leather wingback chair identical to the one in which he was seated.

"Ryder Currin is trying to destroy me, as sure as I'm sitting here looking at you." Sterling pointed a finger emphatically.

"Ryder Currin?" Roarke repeated the name, but more quietly after his father shushed him. The two men had been rivals for as long as Roarke could remember. And with the latest chapter of the Texas Cattleman's Club being established in Houston, both men were vying for leadership roles. Then, there was the fact that his sister Angela was seeing the man. "Look, I know there's no love lost between you two, but do you honestly think he'd go to such lengths to ruin you?"

"Do you honestly believe it's a coincidence that all of this is happening when I'm making a bid to be president of the Houston branch of the Texas Cattleman's Club?" Sterling retorted.

His father went to the bar and poured them both a glass of whiskey. Roarke accepted it gratefully and sipped. The tension in his neck melted a little as heat from the premium whiskey spread through his body.

"First, Ryder Currin takes a sudden liking to my girl out there." Sterling nodded toward the door. "Next, I'm accused of running a goddamn Ponzi scheme. Then a dead body is found at my construction site." He took a long pull of his whiskey, then set the glass down hard on a nearby side table. "No, sir. Ain't no way this is all a coincidence."

"I'll grant you that," Roarke acknowledged, taking another sip of his whiskey. "And it may very well be connected to the Texas Cattleman's Club coming here to Houston. But it's a long stretch to accuse Ryder Currin of being behind it all."

"Why am I not surprised that you'd take his side?"

Sterling groused, grabbing the bottle of whiskey and refilling his glass.

"I'm not taking his side, Ster—" Roarke inhaled a deep breath, then released it. "I'm not taking his side. But I won't accuse a man of such serious crimes without a shred of proof. If we go to the prosecutor with a hunch and some conjecture, we'll get our asses handed to us. You're out right now—" Roarke pointed to his father with the same hand in which he held his glass of whiskey "—because I had provable facts when I contacted the prosecutors and investigators on this case. We'll find a way to exonerate you of these false charges and clear your name. But we do it the right way. That's the only way this works. Got it?"

The old man shrugged and rubbed a hand over his head. "Fine. We'll do things your way. For now."

"Good." It was the best Roarke could hope for. He drained the remainder of his whiskey and stood. "Now, I'm starving and I'm pretty sure I smell fried chicken. Oh, and there's pie."

"What kind?" Sterling asked.

A half grin curled Roarke's mouth. "Texas pecan fudge from Farrah's."

Sterling nodded approvingly. "Sounds good."

Maybe he'd found the key to enduring the next three days with his father. A vat of premium whiskey and a whole lot of pecan fudge pie.

Roarke made his way upstairs, where his bag had already been taken, to get ready for dinner. But he couldn't get the image of the gorgeous woman he'd encountered in the line at Farrah's out of his head.

Three

Ryder Currin slid into a booth at Farrah's Coffee Shop across from Angela and her brother, Roarke. He'd had the results of the paternity test delivered to his office at Currin Oil. They'd arrived a few hours earlier, but he hadn't bothered to open the envelope. He knew full well what the test would reveal.

"Thought you'd want the honors." Ryder shoved the large white envelope across the table to Angela.

Her hands were trembling as she picked the envelope up and handed it to Roarke. "Actually, Roarke, I think you should be the one to open it."

Her brother ripped the envelope open unceremoniously and scanned its contents. Roarke's gaze met his as he slid the paper to his sister.

Angela's blue eyes quickly skimmed the document in search of the answer she so desperately needed.

"There is no way the two of you are biologically related." She squeezed her brother's hand briefly, then turned her attention to Ryder. "I owe you quite the apology."

"Sounds like my cue to leave." Roarke stood suddenly. Unlike his sister, who was elated by the news, Roarke seemed neither relieved nor disappointed by the paternity results. His expression was unreadable. "I have a few people to talk to about…a case I'm working on while I'm here." He leaned down to kiss his sister's cheek, then shook Ryder's hand and left the shop.

"I don't even know where to begin," Angela said once they were alone at the table. "*Sorry* seems like such an inadequate word."

"Maybe start with the fact that you should've believed me when I told you I never laid a hand on your mother that way." The muscles in his jaw tensed.

As a young hand working for Angela's wealthy grandfather, Harrington York, on what was now called the Perry Ranch, he'd had a boyish crush on her mother, Tamara. A woman ten years his senior. They were friends, but nothing had ever happened between them.

Both hurt and anger flared in Ryder's chest. He was aggrieved by Angela's lack of trust. He cared for her deeply. More so than he'd cared for any woman since cancer had taken away his wife Elinah thirteen years ago.

He'd met Elinah, his second wife, during a project in Kenya. And she'd been the love of his life. He was grateful for the years he'd had with Elinah. They'd had his middle child, Annabel, and adopted a second daughter, Maya. And they'd been incredibly happy together for a little more than a decade.

But then his world had been shattered.

Ryder had doubted he'd ever find love like that again. How could anyone even come close to what he'd felt for his late wife?

But then he'd gotten to know Angela Perry as they kept running into each other at various events related to bringing the Texas Cattleman's Club to Houston. And for the first time, he felt hopeful that finding love again was possible.

They'd both been smitten enough to pursue the relationship, despite their last names being like oil and water.

She was the daughter of his enemy. A man who'd wronged him at every turn for more than twenty-five years. By all accounts, he should have distrusted her, too.

But Angela was nothing like Sterling Perry. And though her stunning beauty and generous spirit sometimes reminded him of Tamara, she was very much her own woman.

A woman he'd suspected he was falling for. But her inability to trust him changed everything. What would happen when the next gossipmonger questioned their relationship? Then there was the reality that Sterling would constantly be in her ear, whispering innuendos and half-truths. Trying to turn her against him. Would Ryder have to dance on hot coals to prove himself every time the wind blew with some new accusation?

"You're right." Angela lowered her voice as she placed her soft, warm hands on his and met his gaze. "You're a good, honest man, Ryder. I should've accepted your word, but—"

"But the great Sterling Perry believed the rumor, so you felt it must've been true." His tone was mocking. Something he hadn't intended.

Angela sighed heavily. "Look, I know you don't like him, but he's my father. Given the history between you two—"

A bitter laugh erupted from Ryder involuntarily as he recalled the ugly history between them. Angela's grandfather, Harrington York, had been fond of him. Upon his death, York bequeathed a prime parcel of land to Ryder that turned out to be oil rich.

Inheriting that land had changed the course of his life. He'd gone from a modest ranch hand to the wealthy owner of an extremely profitable oil company. But Sterling, insistent that he should've inherited the land and jealous of the friendship Ryder had with Tamara, had tried to dispute the will.

It'd been nearly three decades since he'd inherited that land from Harrington York. And yet, Sterling still pulled every dirty trick he could to interfere with the success of Ryder's company and to muddy his reputation.

"I don't blame you for thinking the worst of him,"

Angela continued, bringing Ryder back to the moment. "But I know my father. He'd never knowingly confirm an awful rumor like this unless he was convinced you were Roarke's biological father."

"I told him, time and again, just like I told you... nothing happened between me and Tamara. Not ever." He slid his hands from beneath hers and rapped the table emphatically with his index finger. "I respected your mother. And though I didn't like the man she chose to marry, I respected their marriage."

"I know, and I'm so sorry I didn't believe you." She clasped her hands atop the table. After a few moments of silence, her eyes met his again. "So where does this leave us?"

"I don't know." It pained him to say those words and to see the sadness it brought to her eyes. But he would always tell her the truth. "I need some time to figure that out."

"I understand." Her gaze didn't meet his as she fidgeted with the rings on her fingers. "I realize how angry you must be with me."

"I'm not angry," Ryder corrected her with a shrug. "I'm just very...disappointed. But maybe this was the dose of reality we needed."

Her big blue eyes widened with panic. "Are you saying—"

"I'm saying that I need time to think about the reality of our situation, and I think you do, too." He leaned across the table and kissed her cheek, then left the coffee shop.

Maybe lightning really did only strike once. And he should be content with his memories of the past.

But as he walked away, all he could think of was how much he looked forward to speaking with Angela at the end of each day. How much he enjoyed her sharp wit, carefree humor and easy laugh. How much he wanted to be with only one woman. The one he had just walked away from.

Annabel paced the floor of her bedroom. Buoyed by Frankie's positive reaction to her plans for Fairy Godmother, she was finally ready to tell her father about the purchase.

Unlike her former fiancé, Mason, neither she nor her older brother, Xander, worked for Currin Oil. Xander worked the land and cared for the animals on Currin Ranch. Under her brother's guidance, the ranch had become increasingly profitable. She'd stumbled into a career as a vlogger while she was in college.

Despite her father's wish that she, her brother and sister work for Currin Oil, he'd come to respect Xander's career choice. But her family still didn't consider what she did to be a viable career.

Why couldn't they respect that she, too, had chosen the path that was right for her?

There was a knock at her door. Her father. She'd told him she needed to speak to him.

"Hey, Dad." Annabel opened her bedroom door and waved him in, a bright smile on her face.

He forced a smile, but looked sullen.

"Is everything okay, Dad?" She joined him in the little seating alcove near the window.

Her father sighed heavily, then brought her up to speed on the accusation Sterling Perry had made that he was the biological father of the man's youngest child. A son.

"Roarke Perry," she repeated the name. It seemed vaguely familiar, but she couldn't place him.

"I wanted you to hear about it from me and to assure you it isn't true. We even took a paternity test." He extended an envelope to her.

"I don't need that." She moved to sit beside him on the sofa. "If you say it isn't true, I believe you. Period."

He draped an arm over her shoulder and planted a kiss on her head. "It means a lot that you're willing to take me at my word, no questions asked."

"I assume that means Angela didn't."

He sighed, but didn't answer.

"I know that must've crushed your ego a bit, but from her perspective… God, the mere possibility of it being true must've been terrifying. Especially when she's got the devil himself in her ear over there," she added under her breath.

"You've got a point there." Her father chuckled. "But I don't see that crotchety old bastard dropping dead anytime soon. So his influence will be an ongoing problem. One I'm not sure I want to deal with."

"Then I guess you have to decide if being with Angela is worth it." She glanced up at him.

"Who's the parent here?" he teased. "I'm supposed to be the one dishing out the sage advice."

"Actually, there are some things I need to tell you."

"What is it, sweetheart?" He tensed.

Annabel turned toward her father and took a deep breath. "The wedding is off."

"But the wedding is just a few weeks away." His eyes widened and lines spanned his forehead. "Did you suddenly get cold feet?"

"I didn't." She stood, pacing the floor. "Mason did."

Anger flared in her father's eyes. "Why would he call off the wedding at this late hour?"

Annabel sat in the chair facing her father and folded her legs, yoga-style. "You know that vote of confidence? I could really use one of those right now, Dad."

Her father sucked in a deep breath, as if preparing himself for impact. He nodded. "All right, Annabel. Let's hear it."

"I purchased some property."

"You bought a house?"

"No. I purchased commercial property for Fairy Godmother. An old salon and the building next door to it. The salon is the perfect space to do the makeovers, and the space next door will house a high-end vintage consignment shop."

"Annabel, you didn't—"

"I know you don't see it as a viable business, Dad. And maybe you're right. But I believe in this idea, and I'm going to try it."

"You're as stubborn as your mother." He smiled faintly and raked his fingers through his hair. "Especially when she believed she was right."

"Exactly." Annabel relaxed a little. "This venture is very important to me. I get to touch people's lives in truly amazing ways, and it makes me happy."

"I take it that Mason doesn't see things that way."

"No." Annabel shook her head. "And he's not willing to compromise. Guess he didn't get the memo. That's what marriage is all about."

"I'll have a little talk with Mason." Her father stood, his features tense.

"I appreciate the offer, Dad. But please don't. It's over." She shrugged. "I'll admit, I was hurt at first, but I've had some time to think about it. Mason and I want very different things from a relationship. This is what's best for me. I'll be fine."

"All right, pumpkin." His forced smile made it obvious he was unconvinced that she didn't need him. He leaned down and kissed her cheek. "But if you need me for any reason, you know I'm here."

"I know. Thanks, Dad." Annabel sank back onto her chair and watched her father leave.

Annabel worried her lower lip with her teeth as she twisted the large engagement ring on her slim finger. Her relationship with Mason had ended so abruptly, she'd barely had time to allow her new reality to register.

She was no longer getting married. A fact that she was surprisingly calm about. Perhaps even relieved.

Annabel slid the ring from her finger and put it in

her jewelry chest. She'd return it to Mason. She had no doubt the jeweler would take it back.

But what about her?

The floor-length champagne-colored designer bridal gown with countless glittering crystals embedded in the organza overlay of the gown had cost nearly fifty thousand dollars. There was the expensive custom wedding band she'd purchased for Mason and all of the money for the reception hall.

Her father had sunk a small fortune into this wedding. And Mason had called the wedding off on a whim in what was essentially a tantrum.

Annabel felt better by the minute about not marrying Mason. But there was no way he was going to just call off the wedding and then walk away scot-free, leaving her family to foot the astronomical bill.

Not if she had anything to say about it.

She plopped on her chair again, turned on the television and scanned the channels. A commercial for Farrah's came on. Annabel smiled thinking of the rich, creamy lemon icebox pie that was her favorite. And of the handsome stranger she'd encountered there earlier that day.

Annabel shrugged off the memory of the man's sexy smile and the penetrating gaze he'd leveled at her, his eyes an intriguing shade of blue.

She was ending one misguided relationship and starting a new brick-and-mortar business on top of the vlog. Another entanglement was the last thing in the world she needed.

But there was no harm in daydreaming about it.

Four

Roarke stood by the bar, sipping scotch and soda as he scanned the historic Crystal Ballroom located in the Rice Hotel in downtown Houston. The venue dated back to 1913 and had soaring thirty-five-foot ceilings, beautiful mahogany French doors and an elegant lobby with gorgeous crystal chandeliers. They'd been there less than an hour and he already had a collection of lipstick imprints on the side of his face, courtesy of older women he hadn't seen since he was in high school.

"Here's where you've been hiding." Angela stood beside him. "Tired of little old ladies kissing your cheek and telling you what a big boy you are now?"

"Very funny, sis." Roarke scrubbed at his face with a damp bar napkin. "I agreed to be your plus-one for tonight. I didn't agree to make out with every retirement-age woman in the room."

"But you're so good at it, little brother." Angela was clearly amused. "Seriously, thank you for coming. Esme, Melinda and Tatiana all had plans tonight."

Tatiana Havery had been one of Angela's best friends for as long as he could remember.

Angela thanked the bartender for her apple martini. She sipped it. "Mmm… That's good."

"I'll have what she's having."

Roarke's attention jolted to the source of the familiar voice. He'd only heard it once, but he'd never forget it.

"Lemon icebox pie," Roarke said as his gaze met her warm brown eyes. Eyes he hadn't been able to forget since he'd seen them in Farrah's Coffee Shop a few days ago.

"Two pies," she responded with a tip of her chin. Her smile lit up the entire room. A smile he could easily get lost in. She turned to his sister. "Angela, it's good to see you."

"Wait… You two know each other?" Roarke's gaze shifted between the two women.

Something in his sister's demeanor changed when the woman from the coffee shop approached. She smiled uneasily as she introduced them. "Roarke, this is Annabel Currin. Annabel, this is my brother, Roarke Perry."

Those big brown eyes widened. "*You're* Roarke Perry?"

"Guilty." He held up his scotch and soda.

The mystery woman was Ryder Currin's daughter. That explained his sister's reaction.

"It's good to see you, too, Annabel. You look beautiful." Angela fidgeted with her bag. "How's your father doing?"

"He's hurt," the woman said pointedly, but her tone and expression softened slightly. "And miserable. He really misses you."

A look of relief passed over his sister's face and the corners of her eyes looked wet. "Please tell him that I miss him, too."

"No way. I'm not the messenger girl." Annabel's tone was kind but firm. "If you want him to know, you're going to have to tell him yourself. You know where to find him."

"I'll keep that in mind." Angela nodded, then walked away.

"Angela," the young woman called. "Please do."

His sister smiled, then disappeared into the crowd.

"ID, please, miss," the bartender said.

Annabel frowned and produced her driver's license from her handbag.

The bartender nodded, then slid the apple martini toward her.

She picked it up and took a sip. "That is good."

Roarke scanned the woman. She was gorgeous in a floor-length blue gown that reminded him of something a Greek goddess would wear. Athena, Artemis or perhaps Aphrodite.

The smooth creamy skin of her back and shoulders gleamed, highlighted with a dusting of glitter that augmented her ethereal beauty. The peekaboo feature at the front of her dress exposed a little of her midriff.

Roarke glanced again at her left hand. The huge rock she'd been sporting a few days earlier was notably absent.

One corner of Annabel's mouth curled in a grin as she took another sip of her martini. She leaned in and whispered, "I don't know if you know this, Two Pies, but you're staring. It's frowned upon in polite society."

"Is *Two Pies* my official rap name?" Roarke straightened his tie, trying his best to mask his amusement.

She laughed, setting her glass on the bar. "I thought it sounded better than Not-My-Brother."

"Oh, so Ryder told you about that, huh?" Roarke signaled for another scotch and soda.

"My dad tries to be as open and honest as he can be with everyone in his life." Her statement implied that his father didn't operate that way. She'd get no argument from him. "Besides, we're not kids anymore. He wanted me and my siblings to be armed with the truth, should we be confronted with the accusation. He offered to show me the paternity test, but I didn't need to see it. I know my father."

"That's how I feel about my mother." He accepted the scotch and soda. "So I didn't believe it, either."

"Well, here's to *not* being siblings." She raised her glass, clinking it with his. "Because that would make this very awkward."

Before he could ask what she meant, she'd pressed

a hand to his chest, lifted onto her toes and placed a soft kiss on his lips.

Roarke froze, startled by her sudden action.

Annabel laughed. "I can't figure out if the kiss was that bad or that good."

"It was good. Definitely…good." Roarke cleared his throat. He took a healthy sip of his drink. "But the other day, I'm pretty sure you were engaged, Lemon Icebox Pie."

"You're quite observant, Two Pies." Something about Annabel's mischievous smile warmed his chest. "You're quite correct. *Were* being the operative word. The chauvinist formerly known as my fiancé called off the wedding."

"If you don't mind my saying so, Thank-God-You're-Not-My-Sister, you seem to be taking the breakup remarkably well."

"I'm mature that way." Her brown eyes sparkled and she barely restrained a laugh. "That and, if I'm being honest, there was a part of me that had slowly begun to realize that I wasn't happy in the relationship."

"When was the wedding scheduled?"

"A few weeks from today." All of the lightness and joviality faded. A flash of anger passed over her face.

"Well, I'm sorry. All jokes aside, I can only imagine how distressing that must be."

She smiled at him sweetly. "Thank you, Roarke."

There was something so enticing about hearing her utter his given name in that soft sweet voice. It made him imagine what it would be like to hear her say it again as he hovered over her.

Roarke shut his eyes briefly and tried to scrub the sound and image from his mind.

He was only in Houston for one more day, then he'd be off to Dallas again. Besides, the object of his infatuation was Ryder Currin's daughter.

Could he possibly make his life any more complicated?

He'd lived his life in a comfortable realm that existed on the corner of sarcastic and serious. He didn't have room in his life for gorgeous women who looked like Greek goddesses, tossed around smart-ass nicknames and randomly kissed strangers.

Besides, Sterling seemed to honestly respect his accomplishment in getting him released on house arrest. And how hard he was working to clear his name. Getting involved with his arch enemy's daughter certainly wouldn't score him any brownie points with the old man.

"Well, it was nice to officially meet you, Annabel." He set his half-finished drink on the bar and wiped a hand on his tuxedo pant leg. "But I'd better check in with Angela and make sure everything is good."

"Of course." Annabel's tongue glided over her full lower lip. She raked her manicured fingernails through the loosened, wavy ends of her hair, tugging it over one shoulder. "Save me a dance later?"

"I look forward to it." Roarke turned and made his way back to the main ballroom and the table where they were seated.

He'd done the right thing walking away. Though what he'd really wanted to do was lean in and steal an unexpected kiss from her this time.

She was young. At least five years his junior. Fresh-faced and idealistic. She'd just broken up with her fiancé. His father hated hers. And he lived in Dallas while she lived in Houston.

He'd made the right decision to turn tail and run.

So why did every step he took away from Annabel Currin feel like he was walking away from the sunshine and into the cold dead of night?

Annabel couldn't believe that the hot dude who had been behind them in the line at Farrah's was Roarke Perry.

During her conversation with her father earlier that week, the name had been vaguely familiar. But she'd had no idea of what a handsome man Sterling Perry's son had become.

She hadn't been blind to the man's good looks when they'd crossed paths at Farrah's. But she and Mason had just called the wedding off. She hadn't even taken her ring off yet. So how incredibly handsome he'd been was merely an observation. But standing there at the bar with him, she couldn't help being drawn in by his charm.

Roarke looked striking in his tuxedo and he smelled divine. So good that she'd wanted to press her nose to his neck and take a whiff of his woodsy, masculine scent.

Even now, she wasn't sure what had possessed her to kiss him.

It was innocent enough, as kisses went. Still, it had sent a shiver down her spine, making her want another and another.

Annabel glanced over at the table where Roarke sat with his sister. After the paternity test, her father hadn't been up to seeing Angela again yet. And Annabel didn't want to push him.

He and Angela were right for each other, she was sure of it. But each of them needed to reach that conclusion on their own.

Her phone buzzed in her clutch and she checked the caller ID.

Mason.

Mason Harrison was the last person in the world she wanted to speak to. She sent the call to voice mail, then tossed the phone back in her bag.

It rang twice more, so finally she answered it.

"You're screening my calls." Mason's words were clipped. His voice vibrated with annoyance, much as it had the day she'd taken him to Fairy Godmother.

"I'd say that's standard ex-fiancée behavior. Wouldn't you?"

"Is it also standard to send your ex an itemized bill?"

A wide smile spread across her face. It almost made her wish she'd been standing in the room with him when he'd opened the invoice.

"When you suddenly call off an engagement less than sixty days before the wedding because of your archaic, misogynistic notions about marriage rather than making a compromise…yes. It certainly should be. Why should I be stuck with all of these expenses when it was you who changed your mind?"

"I'm not paying for the stuff on this list, Annabel. Not any of it. And I have no intention of compromising on that, either."

Mason ended the call and she was glad. Less than five minutes on the phone with him and she was tense and anxious.

She would never admit it to him, but she should thank Mason Harrison for saving her from certain misery.

Annabel set her empty martini glass on the bar and moved toward the ballroom, mingling with the crowd. She'd wanted to delay the inevitable questions about the canceling of her engagement, but in their circles, news traveled quickly. Bad news, especially.

She put on her biggest smile, tipped her chin and made her way directly toward dear sweet, kind-hearted, generous-to-a-fault Lavinia Cardwell. The gossip queen among Houston's filthy rich and influential set.

Why spend her night retelling the story of her and Mason's breakup when she could just tell Lavinia and watch her work her magic instead?

Besides, with the heat of Roarke's stare warming her skin, she could think of much better ways to spend the evening.

Roarke listened politely to the conversation around him, nodding when appropriate. But his mind kept drifting to the stunning beauty in the slate blue dress who moved about the room. She was all easiness and smiles. Giving no indication that she'd been unceremoniously dumped not too long ago.

And though he'd tried his best to be subtle as he'd sought a glimpse of her now and again, it seemed that she caught him staring nearly every time.

"You're quite taken with Annabel Currin," Angela whispered as she gently elbowed him below the table. "Not that I blame you. She's a very pretty girl. And there's something about her that makes her ridiculously charming. I never understood what she saw in the snobby exec that works for her father."

"Her ex works for Currin Oil?" He raised a brow as he turned to face his sister. "Breaking the heart of the boss's little girl seems like a bad career move."

"Especially one rumored to have his sights set on being CEO of the company one day. If you ask me, marrying the boss's daughter was his way of ensuring that it happened."

"The guy sounds like a real gem." Roarke gritted his teeth. "Looks like he did Annabel a favor by backing out of the wedding."

"Some would agree." Angela glanced over at Annabel, who seemed to be reassuring some overly concerned older woman that she was just fine. "Myself included."

"If the guy is so awful, why'd she agree to marry him in the first place?"

"Because he's all charm and polish on the outside. You don't taste the worm and rot until you've taken a healthy bite of the apple." Angela opened her purse and took a peek into her compact. She looked up from her reflection and regarded his slack-jawed expression. "Don't look so surprised, little brother. I've known guys like that. In fact, I've dated more than a few. And in some ways—"

"You could just as easily be describing our father," he muttered.

Sterling Perry was all flash and no substance. Their mother had married him because of that charm and a desire to please her father, who'd considered them a good match. She'd remained in their unhappy marriage for the sake of her children.

Roarke was glad Annabel hadn't met a similar fate. Though the spirited young woman he'd sparred with tonight certainly didn't strike him as someone who would suffer in silence in a miserable marriage.

Perhaps her ex had come to realize that, too.

His gaze drifted toward Annabel again. Despite knowing all of the reasons he should be content to admire her from a distance, Roarke eagerly anticipated his next encounter with Annabel Currin.

Five

With the business of the event completed, the band had started to play. The dance floor had been crowded ever since.

Roarke had danced with several of the widowed women there, at their behest. Finally, his sister had cut in before Lavinia could ask him to dance a third time.

"Thanks for the rescue, sis." He sighed in relief.

"It looks like Annabel needs rescuing, too." Angela nodded toward his new lemon icebox pie–loving friend.

She was surrounded by a few women plying her with questions. Annabel looked like she was plotting her escape.

"Why do you seem insistent on seeing me with Annabel Currin?" he asked.

"You two have been making eyes at each other all night. I'm just calling balls and strikes here, little brother. Besides, maybe I don't want to be the only Perry accused of consorting with the enemy."

"Don't worry, Ang. You could give birth to a baseball team of little Currins and Sterling would still be disappointed in me." He laughed bitterly, ignoring the twisting in his gut at the truth of those words.

"Roarke, why don't you show Dad the paternity test? Put any crazy notions of you being Ryder's son to bed once and for all?"

He shrugged. "Won't change the past twenty-eight years, will it, Ang?"

His sister sighed heavily. The pain she felt for him was visible in her blue eyes. "Dad is seventy, Roarke. Maybe he'll outlive us all. But that doesn't mean you two have to spend the next twenty-eight years as mortal enemies. Besides, once he's gone—"

"I'll think about it, Ang. That's all I'm promising."

"And that's all I ask. Now, it's been a long day, and I'm a bit tired. I'm going to take a car service home."

"No need. I plan to spend the night at my beach house in Galveston. I just want to make sure everything's okay. I'm as ready to get out of here as you are."

"So, Two Pies, does that mean you're not a man of your word? After all, you did promise me a dance."

Roarke turned his head at the sound of Annabel's voice. She beamed at him, her brown eyes twinkling.

"You could've told me she was coming this way," he whispered in his sister's ear.

She laughed and kissed his cheek. "Good night, little brother. Enjoy your night at the beach."

Roarke ignored his sister's teasing tone. He turned toward Annabel instead and extended his open palm.

She placed her delicate hand in his much larger one and stepped closer.

He pressed his hand to the small of her back. His thumb grazed the soft bare skin, exposed by the low cut of the dress.

"So Lemon Ice… You don't mind if I call you that for short, do you?" He held back a smirk.

"Now, that's a good rapper name." She laughed. "I don't mind at all. Or, if you don't mind being completely pedestrian, we could simply use each other's given names. After all, our parents probably put a lot of thought into them."

"Fair enough, Annabel," he said as they swayed together on the dance floor. "So, tell me about yourself."

"You already know I'm a Currin. I'm the middle child, the official family peacekeeper and a rebel with a cause. I'm twenty-three, a fashion vlogger and newly single."

"You don't work for your father at Currin Oil?"

"I appreciate Currin Oil and the great privilege it's afforded our family. But it isn't where my passions lie. Thankfully, my father hasn't pressured me to join the business the way he once pressed my older brother."

"Xander, right?" Roarke vaguely remembered her older brother. He was just a few years behind him in age.

"Yes. My dad had hoped Xander would take over Currin Oil someday. Secretly, he probably still does. But my brother is much happier running the ranch. And he's amazing at it. So I don't see that changing anytime soon. And what about you? You don't work for your father, either."

"Been asking about me?"

"Didn't need to. Your sister is pretty proud of you. Angela has been bragging about her little brother, the attorney. A crusader for underdogs everywhere."

"Angela said that?" Roarke was genuinely surprised. Most of his discussions with Angela about his career consisted of her trying to persuade him to return to Houston and work for Perry Holdings. "Well, it's nice that someone in my family respects the work I do."

"I understand how you feel." She regarded him with a frown and pain in her eyes. "My father doesn't press me to join Currin Oil. But he doesn't consider the work I do to be a real job, either." She lowered her gaze. "They think it's just a way for me to score free clothes and the occasional trip."

Roarke could feel the tension in her back beneath his fingertips. He whispered in her ear, "Breathe, Annabel. Just *breathe*. You can't allow other people's expectations to dictate what you do with your life or your self-worth." He held her a bit closer. "It's rule number one in the rebel's handbook."

Annabel released a noisy sigh and nodded. "You're right. Sometimes I forget."

The song ended and they both stood in silence momentarily.

"Thank you for the dance," she said finally.

"My pleasure." He shoved his hands in his pockets.

Annabel was gorgeous and sweet. But he wasn't in the market for a long-distance relationship. And any attachment they formed would be an added source of contention between their fathers.

Besides, she wasn't ready for another relationship. She was barely out of her hastily called-off engagement.

But her unexpected kiss had been nice. He'd been thinking of it all evening. And about the possibility of kissing her again.

The opening chords of a popular, up-tempo song started suddenly.

Roarke didn't dance.

Swaying to a few slow songs, he could handle. Anything beyond that tapped into a gene he apparently hadn't been given.

He pressed a quick kiss to her cheek. "Good night, Annabel."

Roarke turned to leave, but her teasing voice halted him.

"Two Pies," she called loudly enough that a few people on the dance floor chuckled.

"Yeah?" He turned around.

"I need some advice about a legal case I'm considering. Could we make an appointment to talk business?" The teasing was gone from her voice.

"You're serious?"

"Very."

"Ryder Currin must have a stable of local lawyers you could consult. Lawyers much better than me."

"Maybe." She shrugged. "But I'd like to work with someone I can trust, and I trust you."

"Why?" Roarke lightly gripped her elbow and guided her off the floor before the drunken party-goer attempting to do the running man crashed into them. "You don't even know me."

"You're using your expensive law degree to defend people who have nothing rather than sitting on the top floor of your father's offices and collecting a healthy salary for doing far less." Her signature confidence had returned. "And I want to deal with someone I know will respect what I do and take me seriously. Not treat me like a petulant child who's wasting their precious time."

"As soon as I leave here, I'm headed to my beach house in Galveston to check on the place." Roarke scrubbed a hand down the side of his face. "Then I'm scheduled to return to Dallas tomorrow evening. Besides, I'm handling a few other cases right now."

"Angela says that you count on a percentage of cases with more affluent clients to balance out your work with clients who can't afford to pay your fee." Annabel raked her fingers through her hair, tugging it over her right shoulder again. "If you agree to represent me, I'll write you a retainer check right now."

Paying clients were always a good thing.

But his practice was in good shape. He didn't need Annabel Currin's money.

Still, he was intrigued. Why did she need a lawyer?

"I'm not a criminal attorney. I specialize in civil law. Are you contemplating a civil lawsuit?"

"Yes." Her eyes flashed with fire and her gaze narrowed. "I intend to sue my former fiancé."

Roarke narrowed his gaze, his brow furrowed. But he didn't laugh or give her the dismissive, incredulous look she feared.

It was a good sign.

He led her over to a table, pulled a chair out for her. The high slit fell open when she sat.

His eyes were immediately drawn to her exposed thigh, but he quickly forced his gaze to meet hers. "Why do you want to sue your ex? If this is a revenge lawsuit, that's not my thing. I'm only interested in seeing that people who've been wronged receive fair restitution."

"I'm not a bitter, jilted bride, if that's what you're thinking." She fidgeted with the clasp on her clutch.

"I don't think anything, Annabel. I just need to understand why you feel you have grounds to sue your ex." His tone was matter-of-fact.

"I'd rather not discuss all of the details here." She glanced around the room. Lavinia Cardwell and a few of her cohorts were staring at the two of them. "There are eyes and ears everywhere."

Roarke's gaze followed hers. Lavinia waved and then turned her attention elsewhere. He sighed. "You're right. This isn't the best place for us to talk. But like I said, I'm heading out to the beach tonight, so—"

"Perfect. We can talk on the way there."

"Wait… You want to ride down to Galveston with me?" Roarke's eyes widened. "You do know I'm staying overnight?"

"It's a rental property, right? I assume you have more than one bedroom?"

"I do, but—"

"Then I'll cancel my room at the Marriott and come to the beach with you instead. We can grab my luggage from the trunk of my car before we leave."

Roarke raked a hand through his dark blond hair, his blue eyes blinking rapidly, as if he was trying to figure out exactly what had happened.

"And for the record, I realize that I kissed you earlier, but this isn't me trying to get you in bed. I promise." She smiled at him sweetly. "I just really need your help, and I realize how limited your time is. So I'm willing to accommodate your schedule."

He tilted his head and rubbed his chin as he assessed her. "I'm a virtual stranger, Annabel. Why would you trust me enough to spend the night at my place in Galveston? Even if we are in separate bedrooms?"

"Roarke, why don't you work for your father?"

"You're avoiding my question."

"No, I'm doing my best to answer it." She leaned forward. "Now, tell me why you chose not to work for Sterling."

Roarke glanced around, then leaned in, replying in a low voice. "We don't see eye to eye about the way he does business. And at the end of the day, I need to feel good about what I do for a living and why I'm doing it."

Annabel nodded approvingly. He'd merely confirmed what she'd strongly suspected. "Yet, you're helping with your father's defense?"

"I am."

"Why?" she asked again.

He drummed his fingers on the table and sighed. "Because I genuinely believe he's innocent. If I thought otherwise, I'd allow justice to take its course. I'd even try to get restitution for all those people who lost their money."

Annabel placed her hand over his. "That's why I trust you, Roarke. You're a genuinely good person." Annabel stood, gathering her clutch and smoothing down her skirt. "I need to talk to Eleanor Evans briefly before we leave, but I'll be ready in ten."

She turned to walk away, but he caught her hand in his. "Make sure someone knows where you'll be. I don't want Ryder thinking I kidnapped his daughter. Preferably, someone who won't make it front-page news by tomorrow morning."

"I'm a big girl. Besides, my father already knows I won't be home tonight." She sighed when he stared at her pointedly without releasing her hand. "*Fine.* I'll text my friend Frankie and let her know where I'll be."

Roarke nodded his approval and let go of her hand.

She walked away, trying to calm the fluttering in her belly at the prospect of spending the next twenty-four hours with the incredibly handsome Roarke Perry.

Six

Angela Perry settled into the back seat of the luxury sedan, confirmed her destination with the driver, then pulled out her cell phone.

She sent a text message to her best friend, Tatiana Havery.

How was the Broadway show?

A few seconds later, her phone buzzed with a response.

Lame. We left during intermission. Melinda and I are having drinks at her place. You should join us after the gala.

A girl's night. It was the perfect time to bring Melinda and Tatiana up-to-date on everything that was going on between her and Ryder.

On my way now.

Angela settled against the seat. There was no need to change the destination with the driver. She and her fraternal twin sister, Melinda, lived in the same high-rise building. Melinda lived on the twenty-fourth floor while her condo was on the fifteenth floor.

There were so many things going through her head right now. How and when should she broach the subject of the paternity test with her father? How would he react? Was there any point in telling him if Roarke didn't want her to and Ryder couldn't forgive her?

She tried to push all of the swirling questions out of her head. But she couldn't stop thinking of how hurt Ryder had looked when she'd practically accused him of having an affair with her mother. The thought haunted her for the rest of the ride.

"Angela, you look amazing!" Tatiana handed her a glass of red wine the second she walked in the door of her twin's condo.

"Thanks, Tee." Angela gratefully accepted the glass of wine from her best friend. "You know me too well. I really needed this."

"Wine?" Melinda asked from the other room.

"And an impromptu girls' night." Angela strode into the living room, tossed her clutch on the coffee table and sank onto the sofa. "So, what are we talking about?"

"Whatever's bothering you." Melinda sipped her drink. "Because something obviously is."

"Is that vodka and club soda?" Angela indicated the carbonated beverage in Melinda's glass, ignoring her sister's comment.

"No, she's been drinking straight club soda all night," Tatiana said accusingly. "Your sister seems hell-bent on staying sober. I think it's because she has some secret she's afraid she'll spill the moment a drop of liquor hits those lips."

"Stop being so dramatic," Melinda griped, swigging her club soda.

Tatiana was just teasing her sister. But the agitation in her fraternal twin's voice and the alarm behind her blue eyes made it clear Melinda was hiding something. Something she wasn't quite ready to discuss.

But then again, so am I.

Melinda set her drink on the table, crossed her legs and tousled her wavy blond hair. "So are you going to tell us why you've been so distracted the past few days? Did something happen with you and Ryder?"

Tatiana's gaze shifted to her and her eyes widened. "So you're the one holding out on me? Trouble in paradise?"

Angela stood and walked over to the wall of windows. She turned back to her sister and friend. "Everything between us had been great. Absolutely perfect. But then I had to go and ruin things."

"You ruined them how?" Melinda asked.

Angela wrapped her arms around her middle. "First, I should tell you about a conversation I had with Lavinia Cardwell."

Angela brought Tatiana and Melinda up to speed on her conversation with Lavinia regarding the rumors about Ryder being Roarke's biological father.

"And you believed her?" Melinda frowned.

"She got the information straight from Dad. Besides, Roarke confirmed Dad's suspicion that he was Ryder's biological son."

"I've heard the rumors," Tatiana admitted, her eyes filled with apology. "I knew you'd both be devastated, so I didn't say anything. But if your own father believes it to be true…maybe you're both being a little naive about whether there was something going on between your mother and Ryder Currin. In which case, isn't it best for you to walk away from the relationship?"

"There was nothing more than friendship between them," Angela said adamantly. "And the paternity test I asked him to take proves it. Roarke isn't Ryder's son."

"I knew it." Melinda breathed a sigh of relief.

"I hate to play Devil's advocate." Tatiana sipped her wine. "But that only proves Roarke isn't Ryder's son. It doesn't prove that he wasn't involved with your mother."

Technically, that was true.

But now that the initial panic had cleared, Angela recognized an important truth. Ryder was far more principled than her father. A flaw she'd chosen to overlook in him since she was a child.

Had her father played a role in ensuring she learned of the rumors? After all, he would do just about anything to break them up.

"Ryder says nothing happened between him and my mother, and I believe him." Angela refilled her wineglass.

"Then why'd you request the paternity test?" Tatiana asked.

"I let Lavinia get in my head, and I wasn't thinking clearly. Ryder is an honest, decent man. I should've trusted him. Now, because I didn't, he doesn't know if he can trust me. I suppose I deserve that."

"Maybe Tatiana is right. Dad will never approve of you and Ryder Currin. Are you really going to allow this man to come between you two?"

Angela stared at her twin sister pointedly as she massaged the band of tension stretching across her forehead, eager to change the subject. "Enough about my drama. What's going on with you, Melinda? You're definitely hiding something. So spill it. *Now.*"

Melinda folded her hands in her lap. "There is a strong possibility that I might be…" She gestured, extending her clasped hands in front of her belly rather than uttering the word.

"You're pregnant?" Angela glanced at the glass of club soda, then back at her sister. "That's why you've been chugging club soda all night."

"Possibly," Melinda reiterated, her voice small and tinny.

Tatiana gaped in response to the revelation.

"You're going to have a baby?" she stammered, her eyes blinking repeatedly.

"Yes." Melinda stood and raked her fingers through her wavy hair. "Maybe."

Angela stared at her sister in disbelief. "You're pregnant by a mobster. Yet, you're telling *me* I should rethink my relationship?"

Angela didn't approve of her sister's relationship with Slade Bartelli, son of notorious mobster Carlo Bartelli. But her sister just wouldn't be swayed.

"Melinda, what are you thinking? It's bad enough you're fooling around with this guy. But do you really want a lifelong tie to a mobster?"

"Slade isn't a mobster." Melinda's face was flushed and her voice trembled. "His father is. Slade isn't involved in the family business. He isn't!" she insisted, in response to Angela's incredulous stare. "He swore to me, and I believe him."

"Let's say he is telling the truth. How long do you think that will last? Eventually, he'll get pulled in, Melinda. They always do."

Her sister wiped angrily at the tears spilling down her cheeks. "I know the situation may not seem ideal to you, but I'm excited about the prospect of being a mother." She placed a protective hand over her belly. "I was beginning to worry that I'd never get this chance."

Angela sighed and wiped the remaining tears from her twin sister's face. "I didn't realize how important this was to you. We've never really talked about it. But still—"

"I appreciate your concern, Angela. But everything will be fine. I promise."

Angela hugged her sister tight. "If this is what you really want, Mel, you know I'm here for you."

"Same." Melinda released her, flashing a grateful smile.

When they glanced over at Tatiana, her eyes glistened and she still appeared to be stunned by the news.

"Tee, are you okay?" Angela asked her friend.

"Yes, of course. I'm just…incredibly happy for Melinda, that's all." Tatiana gathered her purse and stood abruptly. "But it's been a really long night. I think I'll head home."

Angela bid her friend a good-night, then spent the rest of the evening trying to wrap her mind around the idea of her twin sister becoming a mother.

Seven

Roarke was more than halfway to Galveston, but Annabel had yet to discuss her proposed lawsuit against her ex-fiancé. Not that Roarke hadn't been enjoying their time together.

Annabel was bright, refreshingly honest and surprisingly observant. She was as persistent as she was sweet. And she wouldn't take no for an answer.

She'd bogarted her way into what was to be a solitary evening. And though he wouldn't admit it to her, the unexpected company was welcome.

"So, are we going to discuss your case or are you going to keep avoiding the subject?" Roarke asked finally.

He caught a glimpse of the wide smile that spread across her lovely face.

"That obvious, huh?"

"I am an attorney," he reminded her. "It's my job to cut through the bullshit and uncover the truth."

"Fair enough." She turned toward him and the thigh-high split in her dress widened, exposing more of her leg.

Eyes on the road, Roarke. Eyes on the road.

"I understand why you're upset with your ex, Annabel. But bringing a lawsuit against him for breach of contract seems like bitter grapes. Unless you have a very good reason. I could see if the money lost was causing your family a financial hardship…"

"It isn't about the money," she said quickly. "It's a matter of principle. Mason is the one who pursued me. Who insisted he wanted to marry me. That he wanted us to make a life together. I fell for him against my better judgment. I supported his career, and I would've continued to do so."

"So what exactly happened between you two?" There was a part of him that wanted to know for reasons that had nothing to do with her case.

Annabel turned toward the window. "I told you that I'm a fashion vlogger. But I also do makeovers through my blog. Often for deserving women who need the boost. Like residents of local women's shelters or breast cancer survivors."

"Sounds admirable." He nodded. "Can't imagine that anyone would take issue with that."

The more he got to know Annabel Currin, the more he realized that though she was free-spirited, she was by no means the spoiled princess one might believe her to be at first blush. She was an ambitious yet charitable entrepreneur.

"All my life, I've kind of been stumbling through. Trying to find my place in this family and in the world. Finally, it dawned on me that what made me the happiest is the makeovers that I've been doing. And just helping everyday women to truly appreciate and own their unique beauty. So I figured out a way to expand on it as a career. I purchased a couple of old buildings not far from Farrah's Coffee Shop and I plan on converting them into Fairy Godmother."

"You didn't consult your fiancé before you purchased the property?"

"Should I have?" She folded her arms. "It's *my* money and *my* career."

"What I'm hearing is that you knew he wouldn't approve, so you chose to ask for forgiveness rather than permission."

"Are you missing the part where I'm a grown-ass woman who doesn't need *permission* from her father or fiancé to make a purchase?"

"Calm down, Lemon Ice." He held up a hand. "I'm on your side here. I'm trying to gauge the situation objectively. We need to determine whether you have a strong enough case to take before a judge or to perhaps get your former fiancé to settle out of court."

She sighed and nodded. "Of course. I'm sorry."

"So what happened when you told…"

"Mason. Mason Harrison."

"So what happened when you told Mason that you'd purchased the buildings?"

"He made it clear that he wanted a full-time, charity-hopping trophy wife, not a woman with a career and interests other than him."

"Then what happened?"

"He gave me an ultimatum. When I refused to get on board with his Stepford Wife plan, he called off our engagement. Just like that." She snapped her fingers. "No real conversation. No willingness to compromise. He just pulled the plug."

There was a lull of silence between them. Despite Annabel's casual approach to the debacle, it was obvious that she was more hurt by her ex's rejection than she was letting on. Maybe more than she was willing to admit to herself.

"I'm sorry to hear about what happened," he said finally. "Are you sure there's no chance that you two will reconcile?"

Another question that was meant as much to satisfy his own curiosity as it was to satisfy his professional interest.

"Positive. This situation forced me to see Mason for who he really is. And he's not the man I want to be with."

"Then you've mutually agreed that marriage isn't right for the two of you?"

"It was Mason who was so insistent that we get married. *He* wanted a big, over-the-top wedding when all I wanted was to get married on the beach. My father sank nearly a hundred grand into giving us a fairy-tale wedding. Mason shouldn't get to just walk away and leave us with a stack of bills."

"You didn't want to get married?"

"I thought we should try living together first." She shrugged. "He insisted that he loved me and that what he wanted more than anything was to spend the rest of our lives together. It was sweet and romantic. I wanted to believe it was true. So I caved."

"You're not the first person in the world to fall for someone who ended up disappointing them, Annabel." He squeezed her hand briefly before returning his hand to the steering wheel. "Don't beat yourself up about it."

"Thank you for hearing me out and for being so compassionate." Annabel shifted on the leather seat. "That's exactly why I want you to represent me rather than one of my father's lawyers."

Roarke tapped rhythmically on the steering wheel as he considered the logistics of taking on Annabel's case. Finally, he nodded. "Okay."

"You'll represent me in the case?" Excitement bubbled beneath her tentative question.

"Yes, but the moment I sense that you're in this purely for revenge—"

"You won't, because I'm not. I promise." Annabel laid a warm hand on his forearm. A jolt of electricity traveled the length of his arm and shot down his spine.

He couldn't help being attracted to this woman, long before she'd leaned in and kissed him earlier that evening.

Roarke was intrigued by and insanely attracted to

Annabel Currin. Maybe the pull was so strong because she was off-limits.

She was too young for him, from the wrong family and lived in the wrong city. He was the wrong man for her and the circumstances just weren't right.

And now she was a client.

"Thank you for doing this, Roarke."

"You're welcome," he said matter-of-factly. "Any particular reason you waited until we were practically at the beach to talk shop?"

"It significantly decreased the likelihood that you'd turn around and head back to Houston." Annabel smiled slyly. "And that would've been a shame. Getting to know you has been a happy distraction for me. And with everything going on with your father, perhaps you could use a happy distraction, too."

So that was the extent of her interest in him. He was a distraction from her problems. Not serious relationship material.

He was glad to hear it, of course. Because he wasn't interested in a relationship, either. Still, his pride was a bit bruised.

"I hope you didn't take that as an insult," she interjected when he hadn't replied. "What I'm trying to say, perhaps a bit awkwardly, is that I like spending time with you."

He couldn't deny that he enjoyed spending time with her, too. But he wouldn't give her the impression that they'd be anything more than lawyer and client.

"That brings up a discussion we need to have. If

we're going to enter into a lawyer–client agreement…
Well, that should be the limit of our relationship."

"Is that your way of letting me down easy, counselor?" Annabel rummaged in her purse for something. But then she changed the subject before he
had a chance to respond. "Got any plans while you're
here?"

"Whenever I come here, the first thing I do is go
for a walk on the beach. Regardless of whether it's
early in the morning or late at night."

"I love walking the beach at night. Mind if I join
you?" She reapplied her lip gloss. Something that
smelled sweet and made her lips shine.

He involuntarily licked his bottom lip, recalling
how sweet her lips had tasted when she'd pressed
them to his. He'd just insisted that they keep their
relationship professional. Yet, all he could think of
was how much he wanted to taste those soft, sweet
lips again.

"If you'd like." He shrugged, as if it didn't matter
one way or the other.

"Perfect." Annabel gave him a knowing glance. As
if she could look straight through him and read his
every intention and desire where she was concerned.
"I look forward to hearing more about your work and
why you chose to do what you do."

"You asked me about that already."

"What you told me was why you didn't want to
work for your father. I get that you want to be proud
of the work you do. But there were dozens of directions in which you could've gone. Many of which are

more lucrative." She checked her phone, then dropped it back in her bag. "So why did you choose to become a crusader for the underdog?"

"I grew up idolizing cowboys and superheroes. But I don't look very good in chaps or tights." He grinned. "This was the only other viable option."

She broke into the most melodious, genuine, contagious laughter. Annabel laughed so long and so hard that he couldn't help laughing, too.

"First," she finally managed, wiping tears from her eyes, "I'd like to see you in chaps and a pair of tights, so I can decide for myself whether or not you look good in them. Something tells me you're a harsher critic of yourself than any woman with a working pair of eyeballs would be."

"Thank you, I think." He smiled.

"Secondly, that's a cute answer and all, but I'll bet the real answer is a far more serious one. I gave away my first Fairy Godmother makeover when I saw a story about a woman who'd lost everything and was living on the street with her kids because of her late husband's medical bills. There was a big fund-raiser for her and she said she was excited, but nervous to return to the corporate world. I wanted to do something, anything, to help reestablish her confidence. She was my first Fairy Godmother client."

"That's a beautiful story, Annabel."

She was so much more than what she seemed on the surface. Roarke was beginning to understand why a man as obsessed with appearances as her fiancé seemed to be would be intimidated by a woman like

Annabel. She was as sweet as she was persistent. Adorably optimistic, but also staunchly undeterred when she believed she was justified.

He couldn't help thinking of his own mother. What would she think of her old friend's daughter?

"We're here." Roarke pulled into the carport of the beach house on stilts that he'd purchased as an investment property. It had direct access to the beach, just over the dunes.

"This is such a cute little place. Do you come here often?" Annabel stepped out of the vehicle with her clutch in hand. She gathered the bottom of her dress in her other hand to keep it off the ground.

"Not nearly as often as I'd like," he admitted. "I bought it as an investment property, but I also hoped that having a place just a few hours away would force me to take some time off and relax a weekend or two each month. But I don't think I've been here since soon after I bought the place a year or so ago."

"So you're a workaholic, then?" She stood beside the trunk while he got out both their overnight bags, hitching one on each shoulder.

"I prefer to think of it as dedicated to my work." He shut the trunk and made his way up the lengthy staircase to the entrance of the home.

He entered the code into a little lockbox, retrieved the keys and opened the door.

The place smelled inviting, like lemon-scented cleaner and fresh laundry. He turned on the light and set both of their bags down on the floor as he surveyed the space.

The lower level was a large open floor plan with a living room and kitchen open to a wall of windows, which provided spectacular light during the day. Right outside the windows, facing the beach, was the deck. There was even a workspace on the lower level, though he'd never used it.

"I love it, Roarke. It's cozy but incredibly cute," Annabel said as she walked through the space.

He led her upstairs and placed her bags in the private bedroom. On the other side of a full bathroom was a loft bedroom with another desk workspace.

"You can take the bedroom." Roarke dragged his fingers through his hair and tried to shake the image from his brain of Annabel waking up in bed with her wavy hair spread out over the pillow and her skin glowing. "I'll take the loft."

"Thank you, Roarke." She leaned in and placed a soft kiss to his cheek, one hand pressed to his chest. "Let me know when you're ready for that walk."

He sank against the wall and released a sigh once the door clicked behind her.

Annabel Currin seemed determined to push his fraying willpower to its very limits.

Eight

Ryder turned off the television and picked up his cell phone. For the past few days, he'd been checking his phone in hopes of receiving a message from Angela. Despite the fact that he'd been the one who declared that they should take a break.

Angela was a proud woman. She was a Perry, for God's sake. Still, there was a part of him that needed to know she missed him as much as he missed her.

There was a text message from Annabel reminding him she wouldn't be home tonight. But since she failed to mention the Marriott hotel, he was fairly certain she'd altered her overnight plans in some way.

He'd been forced to learn the fine art of reading between the lines of Annabel's text messages in the years following her mother's death. She was now twenty-three years old. Yet, he still worried about her. And he couldn't help wondering where his daughter was spending the night at a time when she must still be feeling heartbroken and vulnerable.

In response to his directly worded text, asking where she was, he received a second message from Annabel.

Don't worry, Dad. I'm at the beach with a friend. Frankie knows exactly where I am. I'm fine. I promise. Love you!

Ryder shook his head and chuckled. Annabel was going to be the death of him. She had a flair for the unexpected.

He wasn't thrilled to hear that she'd purchased a couple of run-down old buildings and had started a business without consulting him. But he admired her gumption. If anyone could make a successful business out of something as nonsensical as playing fairy godmother and doing some makeovers, it was his middle child.

Ryder gripped the phone rather than returning it to the table. He took a deep breath, then dialed Angela's number.

The phone rang several times. He wondered if she was still at the gala. The one they had planned to attend together as a proper date. He was about to end the call when suddenly her sweet voice came through the line, hesitant and tentative.

"Ryder, I didn't expect to hear from you tonight."

He hadn't expected to call. But the need to hear her voice and to know that she was okay had been too strong.

"I know," he said quietly. "I just… Well, I really needed to hear your voice is all." He cleared his throat to fill the silence that stretched between them. "So how was the gala?"

"Good. The usual, I guess. You know how these things go."

"I do." His mind reached for something else to say to keep her on the line. "By the way, I thought you should know I told Annabel and Xander about the rumors and the paternity test. I didn't want them to be blindsided."

"I wish my father had had the insight to do the same. Then I wouldn't have reacted so poorly when I first heard them from Lavinia." She sighed. "And I did react poorly. I stormed into your house, accusing you of God knows what, barely giving you a chance to talk. I shouldn't have done that. I should've known that you weren't that kind of man. And that, despite their disagreements, my mother would never have passed off another man's child as my father's. I wasn't fair to you or my mother's memory, and I'm sorry. I only hope that one day you can forgive me for that. Or at least understand how devastating the prospect of it being true was to me."

"I do," he said quickly. Before she could hang up the phone.

"You forgive me, or you understand why I completely lost it over the possibility of you being my brother's father?"

"Both." He sighed.

"Does that mean…"

"I don't know what it means yet. Other than the fact that I've been missing you every moment that we've been separated."

The line was silent for a moment. Finally, Angela responded, "Me, too."

"Well, that's mighty good to hear." His heart danced in his chest. They'd hit a snag in their relationship, but he couldn't deny his feelings for her.

Falling for someone who wasn't the daughter of his sworn enemy would've surely made his life much simpler. But Angela was the first woman, since he'd lost Elinah, who'd made him want to open his heart again and explore the possibility of love.

"I realize that it's late," Angela said. "But if you wanted to come over, I could show you just how sorry I am that I ever doubted you."

Ryder chuckled. "Darling, I'll be there before you know it."

He grabbed his keys and left a note on the counter for Annabel.

Annabel stared out at the dark water and enjoyed the cool salty sea breeze as she stood on the beach in her bare feet beside Roarke Perry.

She'd traded her elegant gown for a pair of cutoff jeans and a tank top. He was wearing an old T-shirt and a pair of well-worn jeans. His dark blond hair rustled in the breeze.

He seemed at peace in a way she hadn't seen him before. Because there was always something about him that made it seem as if the entire world were weighing on his shoulders. A hazard, she imagined, of being raised by a man who believed he'd been fathered by the man he hated more than any other.

Yet, despite the world-weariness that hung about his shoulders, there was something about Roarke that had captured her attention the moment she'd laid eyes on him at the coffee shop. She'd dismissed it because the break of her engagement to Mason had been so new. And she'd only broken the news of its dissolution to her friend Frankie just minutes before. But when she'd encountered him again at the gala just a few days later, she'd been even more sure there was something special about him. Something that made her determined to get to know him. Despite his last name and the false rumors regarding her father.

Rumors that had easily been disproven.

"I see why you chose this house. This spot on the beach is a slice of heaven." She slipped her hand in his.

He seemed startled initially, but he tightened his grip on her hand and shoved the other in his pocket. "You're right. The house is nice enough, and I can always upgrade the finishes later, if I'd like. But this view and this peaceful little spot… I fell in love with it right away."

"I can't believe you don't spend more time here.

You have not one, but two workspaces inside. It's the perfect spot for a working vacation."

"That's the lie I told myself when I bought the place." He chuckled. "Maybe eventually, I will come out here on weekends. That way, even if I'm working, at least I'll have a beautiful view."

"You should." They walked for a while in silence until she shoved him with her shoulder. "You know all about me and my horrible relationship choices. What about you?"

"Not much to tell." He turned and walked back in the direction of the house, still holding her hand. "I'm not involved with anyone and I haven't been in some time."

"You're easy on the eyes, you have the right job title and you're from a prestigious family. So there's no shortage of women after you." It wasn't a question and he didn't object. "So why is it that you've chosen not to get involved with anyone?"

"Wouldn't be fair when I'm pretty much married to my work." He shrugged.

"You mean you have yet to meet a woman whom you find more compelling than your work."

"Do you always just cut to the chase and say exactly what you're thinking, Annabel Currin?" He stopped and turned to her, studying her expression in the moonlight.

"I find it best, whenever possible." She grinned. "Saves time and aggravation. If you don't count the fact that people are sometimes aggravated by my stating the truth plainly."

"There is that." He chuckled. "The truth sometimes hurts."

He turned and started to walk again, her hand still firmly in his as they cut through the dunes and approached the house.

"It does," she said quietly, the humor suddenly gone from her voice.

If she'd been as honest with herself as she was with everyone else, she would've realized things would never have worked out between her and Mason.

"Hey." Roarke stopped at the bottom of the staircase and squeezed her hand. His warm gaze met hers. "Everything okay, beautiful?"

Annabel lowered her gaze, her cheeks warm. Butterflies flitted in her belly.

There was something about Roarke Perry that was so damn appealing. His warm honeyed voice and the genuine concern in his blue eyes wrapped her in a sense of deep comfort. The kind Mason had never made her feel.

"I'm fine. I…" She couldn't tear her gaze away from his mouth. Couldn't stop thinking of how his lips had felt against hers for even the briefest moment when she'd kissed him earlier that night.

She tugged her lower lip between her teeth and tried to control the shallow little breaths that made her chest rise and fall rapidly.

Roarke tilted his head and closed the space between them, pressing his mouth to hers in a tentative kiss that sent a shiver down her spine and caused a slow burn low in her belly.

Roarke slipped his arms around her waist and tugged her closer, till their bodies were flush.

She gripped the fabric of his shirt and tilted her head, her lips parting to meet his. Annabel sighed softly as he slid his firm tongue between her lips, gliding it along hers as he deepened their kiss.

Her nipples pricked and liquid pooled between her thighs, her desire for him growing. Like a tiny flame fanned into a raging, out-of-control fire.

Suddenly, the sound of voices and laughter approaching from down the beach pulled them both out of the daze they'd fallen under. He pulled his mouth from hers, both of them still breathing heavily.

"Annabel, I'm sorry. I didn't mean to—"

"Maybe we should go inside." Annabel trotted up the long, wooden staircase and waited for him to open the door.

She didn't want to hear Roarke's apology. He'd just given her the most amazing kiss. The last thing she wanted to hear was that he believed it was a mistake, when what she wanted was more.

More of his kiss. More of his touch. To spend the night in the comfort of his strong arms.

Roarke opened the door and extended a hand, indicating she should enter first.

Annabel grabbed a bottle of water from the fridge. Then she called good-night over her shoulder as she ascended the narrow spiral staircase to her room.

She flopped down on the mattress in the dark and stared at the ceiling, her heart still racing.

* * *

Roarke sank onto the sofa and scanned television stations in search of something tolerable to watch. He settled on a home renovation show hosted by a husband-and-wife team with four adorable little kids.

He'd hoped that the discussion of changing roof-lines and possible loadbearing walls would cool down the fire raging inside him that made him feel like he was going to combust. The ice-cold bottle of water on his lap had helped abate the raging hard-on he'd been left with. But he couldn't stop thinking of that kiss and how her mouth had tasted. Or how the smooth skin of her back had felt beneath his palms as he'd glided them up her back, beneath the little tank top she wore sans bra.

Roarke sighed, angry with himself for almost breaking his number one rule.

When he'd started his law practice, he'd drafted a set of personal conduct rules for himself. It was his way of ensuring he would never become the kind of businessman who played fast and loose with ethics, as his father, Sterling Perry, did.

Do Not Sleep With Clients was at the top of the list.

Besides, Annabel had just gone through a breakup. Whether or not she was willing to admit it, even to herself, she had to be experiencing some level of vulnerability. And maybe a bit of fear that she'd bitten off more than she could chew with her new business.

He wouldn't take advantage of Annabel. Wouldn't capitalize on the volatile mix of emotions she must be feeling.

No matter how much he wanted her.

Roarke turned off the television, went upstairs, stripped out of his clothes and took a cold shower. He fell into bed, exhausted. Still, he was unable to sleep.

The kiss he and Annabel shared played over and over again in his restless mind.

Nine

Roarke awakened to the smell of coffee and frying bacon and the sound of pots clattering in the kitchen below.

Annabel.

He checked his watch. It was well after nine in the morning. Much later than he'd intended to sleep, but then again by the time he'd finally drifted off, it'd been nearly 4:00 a.m.

Roarke scrambled out of bed, threw on a shirt and a pair of basketball shorts. He stumbled into the bathroom to find Annabel's toothbrush and skincare products. Her bottle of shower gel sat on the side of the tub.

There was something oddly intimate about standing in the tiny bathroom where she'd obviously already showered and gotten ready for the day.

He made his way down to the kitchen a few minutes later.

"Good morning, sleepyhead." A broad smile spread across Annabel's face and lit her brown eyes. "A few more hours and I was going to hold a mirror under your nose to make sure you were still breathing."

She wore a short white belted dress in a crocheted pattern and a pair of sandals with little tiny bells on them. Her hair was swept up into a loose topknot that shifted when she moved.

God, was she beautiful, standing there in his kitchen with the sunlight streaming on her face.

"Good morning, Annabel. You slept well, I take it?"

"I did. And I hope you don't mind, but you were dead to the world earlier this morning, so I borrowed the keys to the rental and made a trip to the general store up the road. I just picked up a few items for breakfast and lunch. I figured we'd be here at least until then."

He was, in fact, the kind of guy who worried about following a rental agreement to the letter. That meant only allowing the designated drivers, per said agreement, to take the wheel. But it was after the fact. What was the point of bringing up a little thing like a contract now?

"No, I don't mind at all." He shrugged. "And you didn't have to make breakfast. We could've gone out somewhere this morning. But everything smells so good," he added quickly. "Can I help with anything?"

"Just grab yourself a cup of coffee. Our waffles should be done shortly, then we can have breakfast on the deck, if you'd like."

His mouth watered as she transferred slices of crispy bacon onto a platter. She caught him staring and took pity on him. She extended the platter toward him.

He gratefully grabbed a slice. Taking a bite, he murmured with delight. There were few things in the world he appreciated more than a perfectly crispy slice of bacon.

"Breakfast out on the deck sounds great."

"What time is your flight back to Dallas?" Annabel checked on the waffles, then closed the lid again.

"I'm switching my flight. I'll return to Dallas on Wednesday or Thursday." He'd decided that sometime during the sleepless night. "That'll give me time to talk to your ex and follow up on a few more leads with my father's case."

"So you aren't leaving today." Annabel smiled. "I hope that means we don't have to hurry back to Houston. I'd love to lie on the beach and get a little sun. Maybe go for a swim."

The thought of Annabel in a swimsuit made his heart thump harder and parts of his lower anatomy pay attention.

"Uh…sure." He shrugged, his brain too preoccupied with the image to come up with a good excuse for why they should hit the road back to Houston as soon as possible. "Why not?"

"Fantastic. I happen to have my swimsuit. I love the water, so I keep it in my travel bag." She poured herself a cup of orange juice and took a sip. "You should join me."

"I thought I'd get a little work in before we hit the road."

"Is there any reason you can't work from the beach? Besides, it's Sunday. Don't you ever take a day off?"

"Not really." He shrugged. "I enjoy what I do, so it doesn't feel so much like work. Besides, the people I fight for are counting on me. For a lot of them, I'm their last hope of getting justice. I don't want to let them down."

"You really are a good guy, aren't you, Roarke?" Her soft lips curved in a sweet smile, her eyes gleaming. "Don't take this the wrong way, but you're like the anti-Sterling Perry."

"No offense taken." Roarke couldn't help laughing. He'd never used that exact phrase, but it was essentially how he ran his business. He'd ask himself what Sterling Perry would do when it came to matters of ethics. Then he'd do the opposite. "That's essentially true."

"It's great that you're so dedicated to your clients. But I don't think any of them would begrudge you a lazy Sunday afternoon, swimming in the ocean with a friend."

The words of his assistant, Marietta, played in his head as he poured himself a cup of coffee.

Find yourself a nice young woman to settle down with, Roarke. You're always fighting for other people's happy endings. You deserve one, too.

Marietta was an older woman who'd been married for more than thirty years and had half a dozen grandchildren. She accused him of running from emotional intimacy. As if he were terrified by the prospect. He wasn't afraid of giving his heart to someone; he was simply a realist.

Why set himself up for disaster?

His parents' marriage was certainly no road map to marital bliss. Even as a boy, he had clearly recognized how unhappy his mother was. And he honestly couldn't remember a single instance in his life when his father had said the words *I love you, son.*

Getting seriously involved and settling down nearly always spelled disaster for someone whose family had a relationship track record as dysfunctional as the Perrys'. His avoidance of relationships was a public service to women everywhere as far as he was concerned.

"Roarke." Annabel's hand on his arm brought him out of his daze. "One waffle or two?"

"Two." He sipped his coffee as she moved about the kitchen, plating their bacon, scrambled eggs and waffles.

They took their plates out onto the deck in the warm August sunshine. A gentle breeze rustled the strands of hair that had loosened and fallen on her shoulder.

It had taken everything in him to stay in his seat, rather than reaching over and tucking the hair behind her ear.

He took a bite of his Belgian waffle. Light and fluffy on the inside and crispy on the outside. She beamed at his involuntary moan.

"I take it that you like the waffles." She put a forkful of waffle and eggs in her mouth.

"Sorry for the caveman manners. It's been a long time since I had homemade waffles, and these are delicious," he mumbled through a mouthful of food.

"When I was a kid, I'd help my mom make breakfast on the weekends. It was one of my favorite times, because I got her all to myself while the rest of my family was still sleeping." Her cheeks rose in a faint smile. "I don't cook much else, but my breakfast game is tight."

Roarke smiled broadly. "It just so happens that breakfast is my favorite meal. In fact, I've been known to eat breakfast for dinner."

"Me, too." She laughed. "Those breakfast-all-day restaurants are my jam."

They ate in silence for a few minutes as they watched the waters lap at the shore and people start to make their way out to the beach.

Finally, he addressed the issue they were both carefully tiptoeing around.

"About last night—"

"If this is about the kiss, we don't need to talk

about it." Annabel frowned, returning her attention to her plate.

"We do, if we're going to be working together."

"You regret it. I don't. End of story." She stood suddenly and picked up her unfinished plate before heading inside.

Annabel scraped the rest of her breakfast down the garbage disposal and rinsed her dishes before arranging them in the dishwasher. She washed and dried her hands, not reacting when the door slid open behind her. When she'd finished at the sink, Roarke was there, blocking the path between her and the stairs.

"Annabel, can we talk about this?" He set his dishes in the sink and grasped her hand before she could walk away.

"I'm pretty clear on the situation, Roarke. What is there for us to discuss?" She looked beyond him, angry with herself for letting him know how bothered she was by his rejection.

"An awful lot." He lifted her chin, gently forcing her gaze to meet his. "So please, hear me out."

She took a step backward, beyond his reach, and folded her arms. Her gaze didn't quite meet his.

Roarke dragged a hand through his annoyingly sexy crop of bedhead. "I'm obviously attracted to you, Annabel. More than I have been to anyone in a very long time."

"Then what's the problem? You know I feel the same."

"You're my client." He sighed, leaning against the

wall behind him. "And quite honestly, even if you weren't, it would be a bad idea for us to get involved."

"Why, Roarke?" She tipped her chin, her heart racing.

"Where do I begin? You're young, bright-eyed and optimistic. And I'm jaded and bitter, because I've seen too much of the ugliness that human beings perpetrate against one another. You live in Houston, I live in Dallas. You're a Currin, I'm a Perry. There will always be people in our circle who'll believe that I'm Ryder's son. Not to mention that you were engaged to another man this time last week." He seemed breathless after running through the lengthy list of reasons.

Valid points, she had to admit.

"Forget everything you just said and answer one question." She stepped closer, her gaze fully meeting his now. "Why are you attracted to me, Roarke?"

He sighed and his hand drifted to her cheek again. "How could I not be, Annabel? You're smart and beautiful. Witty. Just cnough of a smart-ass. And when I'm with you, I don't feel quitc so bitter and jaded. I feel…light. Happy. Like the world is full of possibilities rather than obstacles."

Her eyes danced as she leaned into his touch. "Well, that's one hell of a first impression."

He chuckled and stroked her cheek with his thumb. "My thoughts exactly."

Annabel fiddled with the buttons of his shirt, her eyes meeting his. "I don't care what anyone else, including our fathers, might think. And I don't see you as being bitter or jaded. I see a man willing to slay dragons for the defenseless, even at great personal cost to himself. A man who gets my warped sense of humor and who is just the right amount of smart-ass, too. You don't often encounter a combination like that."

She rose onto her toes and pressed a kiss to the corner of his mouth.

He brushed his lips over her cheek, then kissed the side of her face. "You're just out of a relationship, Annabel," he whispered, his warm breath on her ear. "You may feel very differently once the smoke clears."

"I won't," she insisted, forcing her eyes to meet his. "Our timing isn't ideal, I know, but there's something special about this that's worth exploring."

He stared at her, and it seemed as if time stood still. He shut his eyes momentarily, then shook his head. "You've already had your heart broken. I won't do it again, no matter how much I want you."

He released her and backed away.

"If that's how you feel." Annabel wrapped her arms around herself in response to the immediate chill that suddenly made her shiver. "Do I still have time to swim?"

"Yes, of course." He nodded, a pained look on his handsome face.

"Then I'll see you on the beach." She slipped past him and hurried up the stairs, her hands shaking.

Later that evening, Roarke pulled his rental beside Annabel's black import in the parking garage near the

Crystal Ballroom in downtown Houston. He got out of the vehicle and retrieved her overnight bag from the cargo area in the back.

The hour-long ride had consisted mostly of silence, punctuated by polite, impersonal conversation or questions about her case.

She'd answered his questions civilly. Had even forced a smile whenever the situation had called for it. But it was very different from the conversation they'd had on the way to Galveston when they'd both been relaxed and eager to get to know one another.

Something deep inside his chest screamed that he was a fool to walk away from the woman who'd made him feel alive in a way he hadn't in so long. But he'd created his code of ethics for a reason, and it had served him well. So he would stay the course.

Annabel popped her trunk, and he put her bag inside before closing the lid.

"I've got your cell number." He patted the phone in his shirt pocket. "I'll update you as soon as I've talked to Mason, all right?"

"Your retainer! I never wrote you that check. I'll do it now." She moved to open her clutch, but he put a hand over hers.

"I know where to find you, so let's just see what happens first. Text me and let me know you got home safely, okay?" He leaned in and pressed a lingering kiss to her cheek.

She turned her head, tilting her chin up, her soft lips brushing his. Annabel pressed a kiss to one corner of his mouth and then the other.

His heart beat faster and his skin flushed with heat. Roarke knew he should pull away. Stop the kiss before it went any further. But he wanted to kiss her again. To taste her sweet lips and hold her in his arms one last time.

His mouth crashed against hers as he slipped his arms around her waist and pulled her against the hard length of his body. He tilted her chin up and her lips parted, allowing his tongue to move against hers. His hands roamed the smooth skin of her back, as he swallowed her soft murmurs and kissed her until they were both gasping for breath.

Roarke broke their kiss, but neither of them stepped out of the embrace. Finally, he heaved a heavy sigh. "Good night, Annabel."

"Roarke…" She held on to him, her eyes meeting his. "Your objections about us… You're assuming I want another serious relationship. What if I don't?"

"You're an all-or-nothing kind of girl." He gave her a pained smile. "I doubt you've ever done anything with less than one hundred percent of your heart."

"Are you a lawyer or a mind reader, Two Pies?" She offered a half-hearted smile.

"Both." He chuckled. Reluctantly, he released her from his embrace. He opened the door of her black, hybrid BMW 330e and she slid behind the wheel.

Roarke watched her drive off, already missing the heat of her body and the sweet taste of her mouth.

Annabel's hands were still shaking and her heart still raced from their kiss. Her brain was flooded with all of the reasons she shouldn't want to get involved with Roarke. And yet, she did.

There really was something truly remarkable about him. Something that made her feel that the world would be a little less palatable without him in it. It seemed ridiculous, she realized. She and Roarke barely knew each other and yet, in some ways, she felt as if she'd known him forever.

Annabel called Frankie on her Bluetooth. As soon as her friend answered, Annabel smiled.

"Frankie, it's me. I just wanted to let you know I'm back from Galveston. Roarke dropped me off at my car. I'm heading home now."

"So," Frankie said, drawing out the word. "How was your stay at the beach last night?"

"We had a lovely time."

Annabel realized she sounded dreamy when she said the words. She couldn't help feeling that way about Roarke. But his insistence that their relationship remain strictly business caused a stone to settle in the pit of her stomach.

"A *lovely* time?" Frankie repeated. "As in…?"

"As in we enjoyed the beach and each other's company, but nothing happened." She couldn't help the sadness in her voice.

"But you wanted something to happen?"

"I wouldn't have been opposed to it," Annabel admitted after a long pause.

"Then Roarke, evidently, was. Did he give you a reason?"

His long list of reasons why he felt they were a bad match scrolled through her brain.

"Lots, actually." She laughed, bitterly.

"Like?" Frankie asked.

She recounted the case Roarke had laid out, starting with their fathers' mutual hatred.

Frankie whistled. "That's a hell of a list. And if I'm being honest, I agree with a few of those."

Annabel didn't respond. She wasn't angry with Frankie for being honest. She was more upset with herself for being so taken with this man.

"Annabel, are you still there?"

"Yes." Her voice was quiet. "So which ones do you think he's right about?"

"It's so soon after your breakup with Mason. You were together for two years. I'm worried that you're not allowing yourself a chance to properly grieve that relationship."

"You think this is a knee-jerk reaction to being dumped by Mason?"

Now Frankie was the one who was silent. Finally, she answered, "It's a possibility. One you should consider."

"I appreciate your honesty. And you've given me something to think about. But I've never been the kind of girl who needs to be in a relationship. I handle being single quite cheerfully. Maybe you're right. Maybe the timing is suspect here. But what if Roarke is the one? Life isn't always so convenient. In fact, in my experience the timing usually sucks."

Frankie laughed. "Hashtag facts."

"So what else do you think Roarke is right about?"

"How will your father take the news if you suddenly become involved with his enemy's son?"

Annabel shrugged. "He's handling his involvement with his enemy's daughter just fine."

"Excellent point," Frankie admitted. "But I thought the two of them broke it off."

A faint smile kissed her lips. "A bump in the road if you ask me. I think he really likes Angela Perry. I haven't seen him this googly-eyed over anyone since my mom."

"You okay with that?" Frankie asked. "Your brother seems pretty ambivalent about it."

Xander was her older half brother. His mother, Penny, was their father's first wife. But they were a poor match and the relationship had ended after a year and a half. And though her father had remained in Xander's life, he'd been raised by his mother in a separate house. Her brother would probably never admit it, but she knew it chafed him that their father considered her mother, Elinah, the love of his life.

Her brother had moved to the ranch full-time when he was fifteen. His mother had died of flu complications just a few years after Annabel lost her mother to cancer. It had been an adjustment period for all of them.

"I know that Xander's mom and your dad weren't together for very long. So it's probably different for him," Frankie continued, filling the awkward silence.

"My mom was the love of my dad's life. Not many people get that even once. If my dad can find true love and happiness a second time around, I certainly don't begrudge him that."

"That's a very mature outlook," Frankie noted.

"Then trust me when I tell you that my attraction to Roarke isn't a rebound/revenge thing. I really, *really* like this guy, Frankie."

"Then I hope you get him." She could hear the smile in her friend's voice.

Annabel was grateful for Frankie's understanding and encouragement. Now she just needed to find a way to convince Roarke.

Ten

Roarke removed his gold-rimmed Maui Jim aviator sunglasses, strolled up to the maître d' station and inquired about Mason Harrison.

The man immediately turned his nose up, as if he'd smelled something as putrid as rotting fish. His demeanor shifted and he regarded Roarke differently. As if by being an associate of the man, he was worthy of a sneer.

"The *gentleman*—" the maître d' emphasized the word in a way that made his disdain for Mason clear "—is at the booth in the back. His regular table." The man indicated the general direction without looking up from the guest list where his attention had returned.

"Thank you." Roarke nodded as he slid his sunglasses into his jacket pocket, then followed the man's directions.

He couldn't blame him for having such a low regard for Mason Harrison. After just a day of learning about the man, he had the same opinion of him. He wondered how Annabel, who seemed to be a generally good judge of character, could've been so wrong about the guy.

Roarke went to the booth near the back of the restaurant. The one that afforded the most privacy. Mason Harrison had his arm draped over the shoulder of a busty blonde.

Roarke stood there, his arms folded as he rocked back on his heels, waiting for the man to notice him.

Mason finally did. He looked up at Roarke menacingly. "Can I help you with something?"

"Why, yes, you can. Thank you for asking." Roarke sat at the opposite end of the curved booth and smiled as good-naturedly as he could manage, given whom he was sitting across from.

"Okay, I'll play." Mason sat back and folded his arms as he stared at Roarke. "What is it that you want?"

"I would like for you to pay your fair share of the expenses from the wedding you abruptly canceled."

"You work for Annabel?" The man's face registered no emotion.

"I'm her attorney, Roarke Perry."

"As in the son of Sterling, The Ponzi Scheme King?" Mason sneered.

Roarke's hands balled into fists beneath the table.

He willed his expression to remain neutral. He wouldn't allow this piece of trash to rile him up and cost his client her claim.

"He's the man falsely accused of running a Ponzi scheme," Roarke replied calmly. He shrugged. "That mistake I'll overlook. But what I can't overlook is the fact that you had the audacity to ask a woman as sweet and kind as Annabel Currin to marry you, given that you've been seeing three other women during the course of the engagement, including Naomi here."

"Mase, is this true?" The blonde turned to Mason, her gray eyes filled with anger. "You have other girlfriends? And you were engaged to be married? When was this?" The woman turned to Roarke for the answer to her last question.

"He was seeing my client for two years and they were engaged for nearly a year."

"You jerk!" The woman shot to her high-heeled feet and poured the oozy red frozen concoction in her glass over Mason's head.

To his credit, he didn't flinch. Nor did he beg the woman's forgiveness or try to explain. "I never said we were exclusive, Naomi," he said matter-of-factly, as if she were the one in the wrong.

"Well, let me tell you, *exclusively*, that you can kiss my ass." The woman grabbed her purse from the table, turned on her heels and stormed off.

Mason picked up the woman's abandoned napkin and wiped as much of the drink as he could from his hair. Almost as an afterthought, he turned to Roarke, who waited patiently for him to notice him again.

"Proud of yourself for causing this little scene?" Mason kept wiping at the mess in his hair. "I've already given my notice with Currin Oil, so threatening my career isn't an option." Mason smirked. "But I suppose that's why you came here instead. So what's your plan? To stalk me and pull a repeat performance with my other female companions?"

Roarke shrugged. "That's up to you, Mr. Harrison. My client has made a reasonable request. Settle with her quietly and you need never see me or her again."

Mason laughed bitterly. "You think a couple of bimbos are worth that kind of money to me?"

"I doubt that they are," Roarke said. "However, I do believe that your reputation is important to you. Both professionally and romantically. You'll need both intact when you target the next heiress whose father's company you'd like to rise in."

Mason scowled.

With con men like Mason Harrison, it was all fun and games until their endgame was jeopardized.

"I'll think about it." Mason wiped the sticky sweet drink from his face and tossed the napkin on the table.

"I wouldn't think too long, *Mase*," Roarke stood and buttoned his jacket again. "I'm not sure how generous Annabel will be feeling once she learns exactly what you've been up to behind her back. I took the liberty of emailing my client's formal request for complete reimbursement of all wedding-related expenses and an apology. You have seven days to respond. On day eight, we file a lawsuit to recover damages in the full amount, plus pain and suffering."

He walked a few steps away, then turned back. "Juries are particularly sympathetic when the defendant is a philandering jerk, trying to get his paws on the inheritance of daddy's little princess. Enjoy the rest of your day."

When Roarke approached the maître d', the man, who was all smiles, cheerfully wished him a good day.

Roarke didn't bother removing his sunglasses as he took the elevator to the eleventh floor of the high-rise building that housed the offices of Perry Holdings. It'd been at least four years since he'd stepped foot inside the company's executive offices.

He made his way down the long, marbled hallway and turned toward his sister's office rather than the large executive office where Sterling typically held court.

Angela's assistant waved Roarke in, informing him that she was waiting for him.

"Roarke." His sister hugged him. She seemed much happier than she'd been the night of the gala. "How are you? I hope you enjoyed your short stay at the beach."

"I did, thanks."

"You really ought to go out there more often." His sister echoed Annabel's admonition.

His mouth pulled into an involuntary smile at the thought of her. "So I've been told."

Angela narrowed her gaze at him as she returned to the seat behind her desk. "Look, I know you're here to talk about Dad's case, but there are a couple of things I'd like to talk to you about first."

He sat in one of the guest chairs facing her desk and crossed an ankle over his knee. "Okay. Shoot."

Angela sighed heavily, a pained expression on her face. "I know you don't believe you should have to show Dad the paternity test, but I disagree. If we can erase this ugly lie he's been harboring all these years, we owe it to him to do it. Not to mention that you've always deserved better, little brother."

He rubbed his jaw and sighed. "He could've asked me for a paternity test at any time. Hell, he could've had one done without my knowledge or Mom's. But he didn't. That tells me that he already knows the truth. It's just an excuse he's been using all these years to be an asshole."

Angela came around the desk and sat in the chair beside him. She placed a hand over his.

"Maybe he's just been terrified to find out for sure. Suspicions are one thing. Having indisputable proof of a betrayal like that…" She sighed. "Maybe it was more than he was prepared to handle."

"I don't really care either way. If he wants proof that I'm his son, he should have the guts to ask me." Roarke frowned, his jaw tight.

Angela removed her hand from his and sifted her fingers through her hair. "If you won't do it for you or for Dad, please do it for me."

"What do you mean?" He turned toward her more fully.

"I mean, Ryder and I stayed up talking all Saturday night and most of the morning. We both really want to make this relationship work. And things would go a lot easier for us…for me, if—"

"If you could prove to Sterling that I'm not Ryder's son." Roarke put both feet on the floor and dragged his fingers through his hair. He shook his head. "Fine. But you tell him. I don't want any part of it. Nor do I expect him to suddenly feel a twinge of conscience about being such a crappy father to me all these years."

"I know that he was tough on you, Roarke. But you willfully think the worst of him. Unfairly so. He might not have been the very best father to you or any of us, but I honestly do believe he tried to make each of us the best we could possibly be."

Roarke gave his sister a look that said they'd simply have to agree to disagree.

"What's the other thing you wanted to talk about?" he asked, eager to change the subject.

Angela's expression softened as she moved to sit on the edge of her desk. "Ryder mentioned that Annabel didn't come home Saturday night after the gala. She said she was going out to the beach with a friend. You wouldn't happen to know anything about that, would you?"

His cheeks heated. "I didn't sleep with Annabel Currin, if that's what you're asking."

Angela shrugged. "I wouldn't expect you to tell

me if you did. I'm just saying…she's the daughter of the man I'm seeing. And an incredibly sweet girl who has already experienced her share of heartache. So for God's sake, Roarke, if you're not serious about this girl—"

"Believe me, Angela, I'm fully aware of the risks here. Which is why I've already made it clear to her that we shouldn't get romantically involved."

Roarke didn't feel comfortable discussing his love life, or lack thereof, with his older sister. Especially not in light of her connection to Annabel's father.

"Oh, my God…" Angela's eyes suddenly widened.

"What?" He sat taller in the chair.

"You *really* like this woman. I thought you two just met."

"We did, essentially. And those were your words, not mine. Annabel Currin is a client. I'm representing her in a civil matter. That's the extent to which I'm willing to discuss this, Ang." Roarke straightened his tie and pulled his phone out of his jacket pocket. "Now, if you don't mind, I'd like to discuss Dad's case."

"So would I."

Roarke and Angela both turned toward the unfamiliar voice.

A tall woman with short dark hair and brown eyes stood in the doorway wearing a dark gray suit.

Two other men hovered just outside the door behind her. All three of them flashed their badges.

"Angela and Roarke Perry, I'm Detective Zoe Warren of the Houston Police Department." She put her badge away. "These two are Special Agent Dalton and Special Agent Rodriguez of the FBI. There's been a break in the case."

"You mean you know who is really behind the financial losses sustained by Perry Holdings' clients?" Roarke stood.

"We're still investigating various leads regarding the Ponzi scheme," Special Agent Rodriguez said. "But that isn't why we're here today. We got a break in the other case."

"What is it?" Roarke leaned forward in the chair.

"We identified the body found at the Texas Cattleman's Club building site," Detective Warren announced. "The victim was Perry Holdings employee Vincent Hamm."

"That isn't possible," Angela objected. "We received a kiss-off text message from Vincent well after the body was discovered. He's in the Caribbean, living out his surfer dream."

"That's certainly what whoever sent those text messages wanted us to believe." The woman studied his sister more closely, gauging her reaction.

Roarke folded his arms. "Vincent Hamm didn't send those messages?"

"That's correct," Detective Warren confirmed.

The detective produced a folded sheet of paper from the inside pocket of her jacket. "You're the lawyer, right?"

Roarke unfolded the paperwork and carefully reviewed the parameters of the search warrant before handing it to his sister.

"They're searching for the phone that was used to fake those messages from Vincent Hamm." Roarke sat on the edge of the chair.

"Here? Why?" The color drained from Angela's face.

"The messages were sent from a device registered to this organization, Ms. Perry," Detective Warren supplied before he could answer.

Angela's eyes widened and she pressed her fingers to her lips.

Roarke shook his head subtly, indicating that she shouldn't volunteer anything further.

"We'll try not to make a mess." Detective Warren pinned Angela with a silent stare. "Ms. Perry, you're the highest-ranking official on the premises. Please remain available in case we have questions or need access to restricted areas of the building."

The woman turned to leave but called over her shoulder, "By the way, I know he isn't here now, but in light of this new information, we'll need to speak to your father again."

"Why?" Angela's voice was strained. "You don't really believe he had anything to do with this, do you?"

"That's what we're trying to find out," Detective Warren said before she disappeared on the other side of the doorway.

Roarke shut the door behind them once the law enforcement officers left.

"They're going to try and pin this all on Dad, aren't they?"

His heavy sigh and lowered gaze was all the confirmation she needed.

Angela's eyes filled with tears and she hugged him tight. "I don't know what's going on or who is trying to frame Dad, but you have to help him, Roarke. *Please.*"

He sighed as he patted his sister's back. "I'll do whatever I can, Ang. I promise."

Eleven

Annabel stood on the sidewalk outside of the soon-to-be Fairy Godmother building in worn cowboy boots, tattered cutoff jean shorts and a faded graphic T-shirt, awaiting the arrival of the next contractor. He would be the third she was meeting with that morning.

She was prepared to meet with as many as she needed to in order to find the right one. Someone who understood the aesthetic that she and her designer were going for and who didn't speak to her like she was a confused "little lady" who needed him to ride roughshod over her in order to get the job done.

She'd promised Mason she would wait until after their honeymoon to begin renovating the properties. Now that the wedding was off, she was eager to dive into her dream venture and document the entire process for her followers on her vlog.

The first post had gone live earlier that morning and already it had more than a thousand likes and hundreds of comments. Most of them cheered her on. Many commenters shared their own stories of past hardships and talked about how much they would've appreciated the kind of service she was going to be offering. Others commended her for her courage in going after her dream, saying she'd inspired them to do the same.

Annabel couldn't have been more thrilled.

An older man driving a late-model truck marked with the name of his construction company pulled up to the building. He stepped out of the truck and smiled at her. His deep brown skin was a perfect contrast to his head full of mostly white curls. He rubbed his whiskered chin before extending a hand to her.

"You must be Annabel Currin. I'm Davis Lewiston." He nodded toward a handsome younger man who'd exited the passenger side of the truck. "And this is my grandson, Elliot."

She shook both of their hands and led them inside the space, explaining her vision and showing them the designer's renderings.

"I love the look you're going with. Classic art deco with a fresh contemporary twist." Elliot scrolled through the images on the tablet that she'd handed him. "What a great way to make use of the remaining art deco design features that are still in excellent shape, like that streamlined black mantel and that banister. The design choices you've selected will really make those original features pop."

Annabel grinned at the approving look on the older man's face as he listened to his grandson.

"And what do you think about the design, Mr. Lewiston?" It was a question she'd asked each of the previous contractors.

"I love the throwback to Old Hollywood." The older man smiled approvingly. "It's a great way to preserve a wonderful old building like this and incorporate it into the renaissance of this neighborhood. I'd like to suggest a few tweaks to the space for the vintage consignment shop, if you're interested."

"By all means." She extended her hand toward the space in question. "Just lead the way."

Forty minutes later, Annabel stood in front of the shop, shaking hands with Davis and Elliot Lewiston again. The older man promised to work up an estimate and get it to her within the next few days.

Barring an exorbitant price tag or some other problem, Annabel intended to hire the Lewistons for the project. They understood what she was trying to achieve and weren't afraid to offer helpful suggestions. But neither man had been condescending.

Fairy Godmother was going to be amazing, and she couldn't wait for the grand opening in a few short months.

Her phone rang. She pulled it from her back pocket and checked the screen.

Roarke Perry.

Annabel grinned as she answered the phone.

"Annabel Currin's House of Pies. What can I do for you?"

Roarke broke into laughter, taking a few moments to collect himself. "You have no idea just how much I needed that laugh."

Annabel furrowed her brow. There was something in his voice that tugged at her heart. "Did something happen?"

"Yes," Roarke said simply, a heaviness in his tone.

"With my claim against Mason or your father's case?"

"Both. Can we meet this afternoon?"

"Yes. And I know just the place."

Roarke slipped into the booth across from Annabel at Farrah's Coffee Shop and smiled. "You ordered me a slice of pecan fudge pie."

"And coffee. I wasn't exactly sure how you wanted it, so I ordered my favorite Sumatran blend. If you don't like it, I won't be insulted. We'll just order whatever you like. But on the phone earlier, you sounded like a man who needed pie and coffee, if not something a lot stronger."

"If only you knew." He sipped some of the coffee. It was a delicious blend.

"Then tell me." She placed her hand over his. "More problems with your father's fraud case?"

Roarke stared briefly at her hand on his. He knew he should discreetly pull his hand from beneath hers rather than encouraging physical contact between them. But when her skin touched his, he felt an instant sense of comfort. One he was unwilling to relinquish.

"Worse. I suspect that he's just become the chief suspect in a murder case. You probably already know about the body found at the Texas Cattleman's Club site."

"Of course. Everyone in Houston knows about it."

"The victim's identity has been confirmed. His name was Vincent Hamm. He worked for my father at Perry Holdings."

"My God, that's awful." She pressed her fingertips to her lips and his gaze lingered there a moment, remembering the sweet taste of her mouth and the softness of her full, lush lips. "But why would the police think your father is a suspect?"

"Someone tried to make it look like Hamm was still alive by sending text messages, supposedly from him, saying that he'd quit and moved to the Caribbean. But someone faked those text messages. In reality, Vincent has been dead the entire time."

"It should be easy enough to prove who the killer is, right? Whomever that phone belongs to must be the killer," Annabel said matter-of-factly.

A knot tightened in the pit of his stomach. "The phone belongs to my father—indirectly. It was purchased by Perry Holdings some time ago. It once belonged to a former employee. A friend of my father's who retired more than a year ago. The phone was never turned off. It's floated around the company since then. And the police found it buried in the back of Hamm's desk."

Annabel squeezed his hand. "I'm sorry, Roarke. But I'm sure the police will find the real culprit soon."

"I wish I was as confident about that as you are." He took another sip of his coffee. "How hard will they be looking for the *real* killer when they seem convinced they've already got the right man?"

He'd like nothing more than to return to his own life and allow HPD to handle the case. But he couldn't just walk away. Not now.

"I'm sure Mr. Perry has the best lawyers money can buy," Annabel said reassuringly.

"He does." Roarke nodded. "But I promised Angela I'd stick around and see what I can find out."

"You're staying in Houston?" Annabel asked, as if she was only mildly interested in the answer, but the widening of her eyes and hopefulness in her tone gave her away.

"I'll be working from my condo here for the next several weeks."

"I didn't realize you had a place in Houston."

"The condo was a present from my father when I graduated from law school. It was his way of trying to guilt me into returning to Houston." Roarke frowned. Sterling Perry was a master of manipulation.

"It obviously didn't work," Annabel noted. "But since you're determined to stay in Dallas, why haven't you sold it?"

"It's a great investment." He shrugged. "The property value keeps rising, and I own it free and clear."

"It's just sitting empty?"

"No, I rent it out through a management company

that specializes in relocating executives. The current tenant just bought a home. She vacated the property on Saturday. A cleaning and maintenance crew has been working on the place for the last couple of days. I'm moving in later tonight. I'll be there until my father's case gets resolved."

"What about your law practice in Dallas?" Annabel prodded, her brown eyes studying him.

"I'll fly to Dallas as needed, to meet with clients or handle legal work. But I'm not taking on any new cases right now. My assistant, Marietta, is fully capable of handling things at the office and a lawyer friend of mine who handles similar cases agreed to help me out. In return, I'll refer any new clients to him for the time being."

"You're a good son." Annabel squeezed his hand again. "Whether he says it or not, I know your father appreciates the sacrifice you're making for him. He's lucky to have you."

He stroked the back of her hand with his thumb.

"You always know just what to say, don't you?" He regarded her fondly, wishing they'd met under more favorable circumstances.

"Now, what happened with Mason that you're trying to avoid telling me?" she asked, breaking the brief silence between them.

Roarke released her hand and rubbed his jaw. "Is it that obvious?"

"Maybe not to everyone." Her faint smile revealed her concern.

This was one of the reasons he'd chosen not to

get involved with a client. He'd been debating how much he should tell Annabel about his encounter with Mason. There was only one reason he was hesitant to tell her the whole unvarnished truth.

He was completely taken with Annabel, and he didn't want to hurt her.

But he was acting as her attorney, so she had the right to know everything he'd learned about Mason Harrison. Despite his overwhelming desire to shield her from the ugly truth.

"Maybe we should order another round of coffee," Roarke said. "This one's on me."

"You're not getting off that easy." Annabel pushed away the remnants of her pie. "If that harrowed look on your face is any indication, I'm going to want dinner and a damn good bottle of wine."

Twelve

Annabel sat up ramrod straight, her back pressed against the leather booth at Farrah's. Her back and jaw tensed and her hands, on her lap beneath the table, had involuntarily curled into fists.

The longer it took Roarke to tell her about Mason, the shallower her breathing became.

"I hired you because I wanted a lawyer who wouldn't treat me like a child by filtering the truth," Annabel said. "Don't disappoint me, cowboy."

"All right." Roarke rubbed his palms on his pant legs beneath the table. "I wanted to catch Mason off guard, so I went to see him while he was off for lunch."

"And?" Her heart beat faster.

"He wasn't alone."

She understood what he meant. Mason had been with a woman. But they weren't together anymore. Why should she care whom Mason Harrison was spending his free time with?

"He's a single man again. He can do as he pleases." Still, she couldn't help being a little angry.

Roarke lowered his gaze to the table, but she caught the conflicted look in his stormy blue eyes. It was as if he were debating whether to give her the full story.

"Tell me the rest, Roarke." It was growing more difficult to retain her I-could-care-less expression. *"Please."*

He tapped the table and nodded, meeting her gaze again. "I've spent the last couple of days doing some research on the guy. He didn't just start seeing the woman I found him with. Nor was she the only woman he'd been seeing while—"

"While we were engaged." She finished the sentence that Roarke was finding it so difficult to say. Her throat suddenly felt dry and her eyes burned. She wiped away unexpected tears.

"I'm sorry, Annabel. I wish it weren't true, and I would've given anything to protect you from this. But you hired me to tell you the truth and you deserve to know." Roarke's tone was contrite. As if he was the one to blame instead of Mason.

This time he reached across the table and took her hand in his, rubbing the back of it with his thumb.

"I'm glad you did." She forced a smile and wiped

away more tears. "It helps to know that it wasn't all in my head, the way he made me believe it was."

Roarke nodded. "Assholes like Mason Harrison always try to manipulate women into believing that. Don't beat yourself up over it, Annabel. This isn't your fault."

"I know." She nodded. "And I needed to hear this. Any reluctance I might've felt about suing him is completely gone. He's lucky that's all I'm doing."

"Don't do anything rash." His brows furrowed. "This jerk isn't worth it."

"If you're concerned that I'm going to key his Mercedes or set fire to his condo, no need to worry. That isn't my style." She forced a smile. "I just meant that I should've asked him to completely reimburse me instead of just paying half."

A wide smile spread across Roarke's face. "I thought you might feel that way. So when I learned about his extracurricular activity, I amended the letter I sent to him. I requested full reimbursement of all the lost deposits and other expenses, including the cost of your wedding dress."

"You *are* a mind reader." Annabel laughed, thinking of their conversation the evening they'd returned from the beach. "I could kiss you, Roarke Perry." The mood seemed to shift slightly when his eyes met hers. "Again."

"So, it appears I owe you dinner," Roarke said after a few moments of uncomfortable silence between them. "Where'd you like to go?"

"Your place for takeout." Her cheeks tightened

in response to the widening of his eyes. "But first, there's something I'd really like to show you."

They walked the short distance back to Fairy God-mother and Annabel showed Roarke the rough space, along with the initial renderings from the designer.

Roarke ran his fingertips along the streamlined, black marble mantel. "It's beautiful and so are these terra-cotta floors." He stooped down and glided his hand over an area of the floor not covered with card-board to protect it. Then he rose and studied the near-est wall. "I wouldn't have thought to keep the glass block walls, but they look amazing in the design."

"I knew I wanted to keep them the moment I saw them." Annabel ran her fingers down the glass blocks with their waves-and-bubbles design.

When she turned back to Roarke, he stood staring at her, his hands shoved in his pockets.

"What is it?" She studied his expression.

"Nothing." His voice was little more than a whis-per. He turned his attention toward the stairs. "I'd love to see the rest. Is it safe for us to go upstairs?"

"It is. In fact, I have a working space up there. Let me show you."

Annabel gave Roarke a tour of the second-floor space that would be turned into private spa rooms. Then at the far end of the hall was the area that would be her office.

"You're already set up in here." He noted the desk and sofa in the room.

"It's a vintage dining room table and the legs have

this cool stepped geometric design. But I fell in love with it, so I'm using it as a desk," Annabel said excitedly. "The sofa I had my brother, Xander, bring here. It was in the barn at our ranch. It'll do for now. This space doesn't really require any major renovations. Just paint and maybe a refresh of the flooring. But we'll worry about that later."

"Sensible." He nodded, looking around the office. "Have you settled on a contractor for the project?"

"Officially? No. But I'm pretty sure I'll be going with the gentleman I met earlier today. He and his grandson have a small company. But I've seen his past work and there was something about them both I really liked."

"I'd be happy to review the contracts before you sign them."

"I'd appreciate that, Roarke." She stepped closer to him. "Thank you."

Roarke didn't move away from her or toward her, and his gaze didn't leave her face. She was sure there was something he wanted to say.

She took another step forward and pressed her hands to his chest, then rose onto her toes.

Roarke slipped his hands around her waist and closed the distance between them. There was a delicious hunger in his kiss that made her entire body ache with desire for him.

Ever since they'd parted ways upon their return from his place at the beach, she hadn't been able to stop thinking of him.

No matter how hard she'd tried, she couldn't forget

his kiss. Couldn't stop replaying the moments they'd shared. Couldn't stop wanting him.

Roarke kissed her harder, his mouth sliding against hers as his palms glided down over her bottom, pulling her against the ridge beneath his zipper.

She gasped at the sensation and Roarke took the opportunity to slip his tongue inside her mouth as he deepened their kiss.

The space between her thighs throbbed and her nipples ached. Annabel honestly couldn't remember ever wanting someone as much as she wanted Roarke Perry.

Annabel pulled away from him, taking a few steps backward until the back of her calves hit the sofa. She pulled her tank top over her head and tossed it aside.

Roarke stared at her, his chest heaving as he loosened his tie and stepped toward her until her body was pinned between his and the sofa.

Annabel looped her arms around his neck, pulling his face toward hers. She kissed the edge of his mouth and whispered in his ear. "I want you, Roarke."

He breathed heavily as his hands glided up her side and grazed her sensitive nipples with his thumbs through the sheer fabric of her black tulle and lace Agent Provocateur bra.

His only response was a bruising openmouthed kiss as his large hands moved to cup either side of her face.

Then his hands slid down to her back where he fumbled with the hooks of her bra, till the sound of a door slamming downstairs halted them.

"Did you lock the door?" he asked.

She shook her head and they both stood motionless, listening for any other sounds.

"Annabel? Are you here?" Frankie called. "Xander brought the chairs you wanted for your office."

"Shit." She uttered the word beneath her breath. "That's my friend and—"

"Your brother. I know." He retrieved her tank top, handing it to her. "Maybe you should go downstairs and meet your friend. I'm kind of…" He indicated the situation below his waist that would make it obvious what they'd been up to.

Or at least what they would've been up to, if not for the interruption.

"Got it." She slipped her shirt on and called downstairs. "I'll be right there, Frankie. Just give me a sec."

Annabel glanced back over her shoulder at Roarke, who'd settled into the chair behind her makeshift desk.

"Sorry, I wasn't expecting company," she whispered. "Come join us whenever you can."

Annabel took a deep breath and made her way downstairs.

Roarke followed the sound of voices down the stairs once he was comfortably able to stand again.

The large man who shared many of Annabel's features immediately frowned when he saw him.

Annabel stopped talking and followed her brother's gaze.

"Xander and Frankie, this is—"

"Roarke Perry. I'm aware." Xander folded his arms and stared him down. "What is he doing here?"

"I'm her lawyer," Roarke offered quickly, clearing his throat. The disappointed look in Annabel's eyes caused a twinge of guilt. "We were discussing some business I'm handling for her."

"Since when is Sterling Perry's son your lawyer?" He turned to his sister.

"Since a few days ago." Annabel ignored her brother's accusatory tone. She turned to Roarke. "Your timing is perfect. Would you mind helping us bring in a few chairs?"

"Not at all." He smiled, despite Xander's frown.

"It's a pleasure to meet you." Frankie held out her hand and he shook it. "Don't mind my fiancé. He's just your typical overprotective older brother. And after what just happened with Mason…"

"I completely understand." Roarke nodded, then followed the three of them out to Xander's pickup truck, where he helped her brother bring in four chairs.

When they'd set the last chair down in Annabel's office, Roarke's phone buzzed. He checked the text message. Angela was ready to tell Sterling about the paternity test. She asked that he come out to the ranch.

Roarke nearly ran over Xander, who stood between him and the open door. Annabel and Frankie had gone back downstairs, leaving the two of them alone.

He honestly didn't have time right now for whatever Xander Currin's problem was with him.

Roarke slid his phone back into his pocket. "Is there something you need to say, Xander?"

"Yeah. I don't know what kind of game your family is trying to run on mine—"

"What the hell are you talking about?" Roarke narrowed his gaze at the man.

"First, your sister starts dating my father. Now, I walk in on you with my little sister doing whatever it is you two were doing up here. And spare me the bullshit about talking business. I'm not buying it."

Roarke didn't respond to the accusation either way. Instead, he addressed Xander's initial concern. One he could categorically deny.

"No one is trying to *run a game* on your family, Xander. My sister and your dad…" He raked a hand through his hair. "I was against it initially, too. But Angela *really* cares for your father. They seem to genuinely make each other happy. And as long as that's the case, I'm happy for them both."

"I accepted my dad and Angela's relationship. Though I'm less inclined to forgive her for not taking him at his word when he told her there was no way he was your father. But now, not a week after her ex called off the wedding, you're all over my sister. I can't help wondering about your timing and your motive. Is Sterling Perry so desperate to get his hands on the oil well he believes he should've inherited from your grandfather that he's sending his children to do his dirty work?"

Roarke was so damned tired of hearing about the oil-rich land that his grandfather had left to Ryder

Currin. The property that Sterling felt should've been left to their family.

"That's what you think this is?" Roarke's face heated and his heart thudded in his chest. "You obviously don't know anything about me. I would never take advantage of Annabel. And unlike my father, I'm glad my grandfather left that land to your dad. My family is incredibly wealthy, even without that piece of property. But for your family it was life-changing."

Xander's gaze softened momentarily, but then he regarded Roarke suspiciously. "All I know is the apple doesn't fall far from the tree."

It wasn't the first time someone who didn't know Roarke had accused him of being like his unscrupulous father.

"Well, in this case it rolled down the hill and onto the neighboring farm. It's why I chose to stay in Dallas after law school. And it's the reason I've always refused to work for Perry Holdings."

Xander's arms dropped to his sides. "Then what the hell are you doing here?"

Annabel burst through the door as if she'd bounded up the stairs the moment she'd realized he and Xander had been left alone together.

"It's none of your business why he's here." She poked her brother in the gut. "So cut it out. I can take care of myself."

Xander scowled. He turned toward Annabel and opened his mouth to object, but she folded her arms and pinned him with a stare. He huffed and headed downstairs without a word.

"Love you, too!" She called down the hall after her brother, then locked her office door. "Sorry about that." Annabel wrapped her arms around Roarke's neck and kissed him. "Would you mind if I took a rain check for dinner?"

"Not at all." He stroked her cheek. "Something just came up that I need to handle. Give me a call when you're ready to reschedule. I'll let you know as soon as I get a response from Mason."

Roarke kissed Annabel and went downstairs, bidding Xander and his fiancée, Frankie, a hasty goodbye.

He'd been disappointed when Xander and Frankie had interrupted them. But it had been for the best. When it came to Annabel, he had zero self-control.

Roarke got behind the wheel of his rental and headed toward the Perry Ranch.

En route, he placed a call to the investigators on Sterling's fraud case. With any luck, they'd made some progress toward clearing his father's name.

Thirteen

Angela Perry paced the floor in her father's den after he'd stepped out of the room to make a phone call.

Despite what her brother said, her father needed to know the truth about Roarke's paternity once and for all. But her reasons for sharing the results with her father weren't solely unselfish. She was serious about Ryder Currin. The more she was with him, the more she could see a future for herself with him. A future that would be filled with anger and animosity if her father still believed such awful lies about the man she cared for so deeply.

"Angela…"

She jumped at the sound of her father's voice, not realizing he'd reentered the room.

He frowned, then poured himself another glass of

whiskey. "You ready to tell me whatever it is that's got you walking around here on eggshells?"

"What do you mean?" She raked her fingers through her hair and sat on the leather sofa.

Sterling sipped his whiskey and sat across from her. "Never known you to hold your tongue when you've got something to say. I don't reckon you should start today. Got a date with my favorite show and the rest of that bottle, so quit dancing around whatever it is and spit it out."

Angela clasped her hands and raised her gaze to meet her father's. She couldn't stall any longer. Sterling's impatience wouldn't allow her to wait for Roarke to arrive. And her brother honestly hadn't wanted to be a part of this conversation anyway. "All right, Dad. I want to talk to you about a few things. First, you know that I've been seeing Ryder."

Sterling grunted and took another swig of his whiskey. "Because you still haven't come to your senses yet," he muttered.

"That isn't fair." She shot to her feet. "You're wrong about him."

"And what exactly is it that I'm wrong about, Angela? About him stealing land that should've gone to this family? The very land that built his fortune?"

"It was Granddad's land and he had every right to leave it to whomever he chose. Besides—" Angela gestured around the opulent space "—it's not as if we're somehow lacking. Look around you, Dad. You have everything you've ever wanted or needed."

"Except that land and the oil well on it." Sterling

hit the table with his fist, causing the whiskey inside his glass to slosh around.

"This isn't really about the land or the oil well on it, is it, Dad?" She folded her arms. "It's about you being one-upped by a younger man who came from nothing. A man you didn't feel was worthy of the things you have. That's why you resent him."

"He didn't deserve that land." He pointed at her. "And he damn sure didn't deserve—" Sterling sighed, settling back in the chair.

"He didn't deserve what, Dad?" She stepped forward when he didn't answer. "He didn't deserve Mom?"

Her father's attention snapped to hers and he frowned. His expression was filled with both anger and pain. "You know about that?"

Angela sank onto the sofa again. "Don't act so surprised, Dad. You talked about this with Lavinia Cardwell, for God's sake. You had to know it would get back to me. Maybe that was the point."

"I always tried my best to shield you kids from the ugly truth." He didn't deny the accusation. "But I see now that was a mistake. Had you known, you would never have gotten involved with that lowlife to begin with."

"Ryder Currin isn't a lowlife, Dad. Nor is he Roarke's father."

"You were too young to know what was going on back then."

"It doesn't matter. I knew Mom. And I know she'd

never have had another man's child and tried to pass him off as yours."

Sterling winced, as if the words had caused him physical pain. "Things aren't always as simple as they seem, Angela. And sometimes the people we love hurt us."

"You're wrong about Mom. And you're wrong about Ryder, too. If he'd thought for one moment that Roarke was his son, he wouldn't have allowed another man to raise him."

Sterling laughed bitterly. "A few months with this man and suddenly you'll believe anything he says over the word of your own father? Talk about a snake oil salesman. I wish I had Ryder Currin's gift for convincing folks that he's innocent and misunderstood." He pointed to his ankle monitor. "Then I wouldn't have this damn thing on my ankle now."

"I regret it now, but I didn't just take Ryder's word for it." Angela rummaged in her purse and pulled out the envelope Ryder had given her at the coffee shop that day. She shoved it into her father's hands. "See for yourself."

Sterling's eyes widened and his mouth fell open. "You asked him to take a paternity test?"

"Yes. I'm not proud of it, but I did."

"And your brother agreed to it?" He didn't open the envelope.

"I think he was finally ready to get some closure on the matter, too. And to understand why you always treated him so cruelly."

"I was never cruel to Roarke." He lowered his gaze

and dropped the envelope on the table. "Was I tough on him? Yes. But that was because he was my only son. I wanted him to be strong enough to handle whatever he'd face in the world. Plus, he was the baby in a family full of women. You all did your best to spoil him rotten. I had to ensure he had the Perry will and strength."

"I don't buy that for a second, Dad. And neither do you. Maybe that was the thing you told yourself so that you could sleep at night. But it certainly didn't help Roarke or your relationship with him."

"That's enough." His face flushed and his jaw tensed. "You don't know what you're talking about."

"I know that your only son refuses to work for you. That he couldn't get out of here fast enough when he turned eighteen. That he hadn't been home in years. Even with all of your recent legal troubles, I had to *beg* him to come home. And I know that you two have talked more in the past couple of weeks than you have in the last five years."

She sat down again in a huff. "You can keep trying to convince yourself otherwise, Dad. But you were wrong about Ryder being Roarke's father. You ruined your relationship with your son and any chance of being truly happy with Mom. And there was never one shred of truth to it."

They sat together in silence, the air heavy between them.

He stared down at the envelope, and for the first time in her memory, her father's hands seemed unsteady.

"You've based an entire lifetime of hurt and pain on a false assumption that you could've disproven at any time by simply asking Roarke to take a paternity test. Hell, when he was a kid, you could've had the test done and he would never have known the reason for it. But you didn't. Now you have absolute, indisputable proof in front of you that he isn't Ryder's son. Yet, you're hesitant to review the results. Why?"

He narrowed his gaze at her and sighed. Finally, he opened the envelope and read the results. He closed his eyes briefly, as an expresson of intense relief passed over his face.

Angela sat on the edge of the table in front of her father.

"Look, Dad, you know how much I love you. I've dedicated my life to supporting Perry Holdings and your dreams for the empire that you've built. But I've finally found someone who truly makes me happy. And I won't let your misguided hatred toward Ryder Currin keep us apart. I hope you can understand that."

"This proves that he isn't Roarke's father. It doesn't prove that he didn't try to take your mother away from me. Nor does it change the fact that I was entitled to—"

"I'm not asking your permission, Dad," Angela said abruptly. "And I won't keep going 'round in circles with you about this. I'm in love with Ryder and I almost lost him because I let you and Lavinia get in my head. And if you can't respect my decision to be with him, you're going to lose me, too. Just like you lost Roarke."

They stared at each other in silence for a few moments.

Her father sighed. "Maybe you're right. Maybe I'm not being fair to Currin. I just don't want to see you get hurt."

Angela squeezed her father's hand. "I don't want that, either. But you taught us to never make decisions based on fear. If I walk away from him because I'm worried about what might happen down the road, I'm always going to regret it."

"Then I hope that Ryder Currin is the man you believe him to be." He leaned in and kissed her cheek. "For your sake."

She hoped so, too.

Fourteen

Roarke parked his rental SUV beside Angela's car and hurried inside the Perry Ranch. He found his father and sister sitting in the den.

He clapped his hands, a broad smile on his face. "I've got great news."

"I've heard." Sterling tapped a large envelope on the coffee table. He recognized it as the paternity test results that Ryder had given them that day at the coffee shop.

"That isn't what I meant."

"Then what's your good news, Roarke?" Angela approached him.

"It's about the fraud case." He turned to Sterling. "I've had my investigators going over the investment documentation of some of your clients who lost big recently, as well as your banking information. This case in no way meets the legal definition of a Ponzi scheme. You didn't guarantee anyone returns and you didn't use the money from new investors to pay out previous investors. The stock was doing quite well until rumors and innuendo sparked investor panic, which then triggered the slide of the stock's value. I shared everything I found with your lawyers."

"Then why haven't the charges been dropped?" Angela asked impatiently.

"The FBI certainly wasn't going to take our documentation at face value. Nor were they in a hurry to prove Dad innocent of fraud. Especially with the murder investigation going on." Roarke went behind the bar to pour himself a scotch and soda. "But I called the agent heading up the fraud case and he said that Ster— Dad will be released from house arrest as soon as they can get someone out here to take that thing off." Roarke nodded toward his father's ankle.

"Thank goodness." Sterling lifted his pant leg and scratched the skin beneath the monitor. "This thing is driving me insane and I've been going stir-crazy in this house. I need to get back to my office as soon as possible. We need to devise a plan to counteract all the bad publicity and the negative impact it's had on our company. I should sue the local police department and the feds for false arrest and the resulting financial losses. There's no guarantee that we'll make those up. At least, not anytime soon."

"Relax, Dad." Angela placed a hand on her father's shoulder. Then she turned to Roarke and hugged him.

"You're a hell of a lawyer, little brother. Thank you." She ruffled his hair.

"Thanks, Ang." He appreciated his sister's heartfelt thanks.

Because he hadn't gone into their family business, he'd often felt the disappointment of not only his father but his sisters, too. So it felt good to be acknowledged for what he'd been able to achieve on his father's behalf.

Sterling approached him, his hand extended. "Yes, by all means, thank you, son. I can't tell you how much I appreciate what you've done for me."

"Glad I could help." Roarke shook his father's hand. "But it's too soon to celebrate. There's still the murder investigation to consider."

"I know." Angela nodded sadly. "Poor Vincent. He might not have been the best employee, but he certainly didn't deserve this."

"They don't honestly believe I had anything to do with that man's death, do they?" Sterling frowned.

"The investigators claim that people inside your company suspect that Vincent stumbled upon your Ponzi scheme and threatened to out you, so you killed him or had him killed. Either way, you've become their chief suspect."

"But you just proved that I wasn't trying to defraud anyone. So what possible motive would I have to kill the man?"

"What if Vincent was the one who started the rumors in the first place?" Angela asked. "The perception that Perry Holdings defrauded investors created substantial losses for our company and our clients. Wouldn't that give Dad just as strong of a motive for shutting Vincent up?"

"Whose side are you on?" Sterling grumbled.

"Yours, of course," she assured him. "But we need to look at this thing from every angle."

"She's right, Dad. It's the only way we can stay ahead of this. We need to think the way they do and anticipate their next move." Roarke sat in the chair and sipped his scotch and soda.

"So what now?" Sterling picked up his glass from the table and drained his whiskey.

"First, we pray that Detective Warren and her team are competent enough to find the real killer, and soon." Roarke set his glass on a coaster on the table. "Second, we keep digging for clues. Find out if anyone might've had an ax to grind with Vincent Hamm. Or you."

Both Sterling and Angela looked alarmed by the possibility. But the truth was that his father collected enemies like some men collected coins or rare stamps. There was a long list of people outside the company, and a few inside, who might want to exact revenge on Sterling Perry. His father could teach a masterclass on rubbing people the wrong way. In his father's case, familiarity often did indeed breed contempt.

It was a lesson he'd learned firsthand.

"How long will you be in Houston?" Angela asked her brother.

"Until this case is settled." Roarke shrugged, as

if it were no big deal. "I've made arrangements with my office in Dallas."

"That's great, Roarke. You know how much I appreciate this, but I can't help wondering if your affinity for a beautiful young lady had a hand in your decision." She smiled. "If so, just remember what we talked about earlier."

His sisters just couldn't resist ribbing him, especially when it came to his love life. "This has nothing to do with Annabel."

"Sure, little brother." Angela's teasing grin made it clear she thought he was full of it. She grabbed her purse. "I'm having dinner with her father tonight. I'll be sure to say hello, if I see her."

"Wait… You're talking about Currin's daughter?" Sterling's gaze shifted from Angela to Roarke, then back again. "This is a big city. Did you two find it absolutely necessary to go swimming in the Currin dating pool?"

Roarke sighed. "Thanks, sis."

"You're welcome," she practically sang as she turned to leave. "Good night."

Roarke finished the last of his drink as an awkward silence settled over the room.

"I'm sure you've had a long day, so I'll just—" Roarke started to rise to his feet.

"Have another drink with your old man?" Sterling asked.

"I'd better not." Roarke rubbed his palms on his pant legs. "I have to drive back to the condo. One Perry in an ankle bracelet is more than enough."

"You've got a point." Sterling chuckled. "But of course, you don't have to go back to the condo tonight. You're welcome to stay. I was just gonna hunker down and watch some old Westerns like we did on Saturday nights when you were a kid."

His mouth curved in an involuntary smile as he recalled those nights when it was just the two of them, watching old spaghetti Westerns starring Clint Eastwood, Charles Bronson, Lee Van Cleef or Henry Fonda. Violent movies his mother preferred that he not watch.

One of the many battles of wills his parents had where he was concerned.

"Sounds like fun, but I—"

"C'mon, son." His father's voice was soft and pleading.

Roarke studied Sterling's expression. For the first time that he could remember, his father didn't look like the imposing giant who ran his empire with a steel fist. The father who only showed softness around the edges where his daughters were concerned.

Sterling Perry looked vulnerable and every bit of his seventy years of age. Maybe more.

"I'd really like it if you'd stay. It'll give us a chance to talk." Sterling stood, grabbing his glass from the table. He picked up Roarke's glass, too. "What are you drinking tonight, son?"

"Scotch and soda." It wasn't lost on him that his father had made a point of calling him *son* repeatedly. "Thanks, Dad."

Sterling took their glasses behind the bar and

poured their drinks. He handed the tumbler to Roarke and returned to his chair. He sipped his drink in silence.

"So, I fully expect that the FBI will drop the charges of fraud related to the allegations of a Ponzi scheme." Roarke set his drink on the table after taking a deep sip. "But until you've been cleared in the murder investigation, it would be best if you lie low."

"Thank you, Roarke. For everything you've done these past few weeks. I know that you've got your own life and your practice back in Dallas. And let's face it, I'm not winning any father-of-the-year awards where you're concerned. I wouldn't have blamed you if you hadn't wanted to get involved. But I'm thankful you did."

"Glad I could help." Roarke nodded, accepting the compliment. It was unfamiliar and uncomfortable for both of them.

"Roarke," Sterling said after a quiet lull between them. "I'm sorry, son. I know I was much harder on you than I was on your sisters. I know you think it's because..." His father glanced down at the envelope on the table, but he couldn't seem to bear to vocalize his thoughts. "It wasn't. At least, I always told myself it wasn't. That I just needed to toughen you up. To make sure you were strong enough to one day stand in my shoes and be the man your sisters will need when you become the patriarch of this family."

Roarke carefully regarded his father's words and his response to them. Over the years, he'd learned to bury his hurt and anger over his father's treatment.

He'd convinced himself that he didn't really give a damn that his father had considered him a letdown. Because he never wanted to be like Sterling Perry, anyway.

But the truth was it had hurt like hell to be a constant disappointment to a man like Sterling Perry. And like any human being, he'd wanted his father to be proud of him.

"I appreciate that you felt you were making me a stronger, more capable man." Roarke sipped his scotch and soda. "But it sure as hell felt extremely personal."

"I know." Lines spanned across Sterling's forehead. "And I wish I could say you were wrong. But I think we both know my actions were colored by what I believed to be true."

"I appreciate your honesty. I really do." Roarke swallowed back the lifetime of pain that bubbled up in his chest. "But if you really believed I was Ryder Currin's son, why didn't you ask for a paternity test when I was born? Or at any time in the past twenty-eight years? You could've saved us both a lot of heartache."

Sterling took a long pull from his glass and set it on the table with a thud. He sighed heavily. "I was terrified it was true. That once I had confirmation, our relationship would never recover."

Roarke fought back the anger and bitterness that burned his lungs. Emotions he'd buried deep.

He ignored the part of himself that wanted to scream and curse. To bang his fists on the table and tell Sterling Perry exactly what he could do with his two-decades-too-late apology.

"I'm sorry, it's late and I have an early-morning conference call about a case I'm working on." Roarke stood abruptly.

"You really don't need to go, son. In fact, I'd appreciate the company."

"The spaghetti Western marathon sounds great. Really. Another night, okay?"

Roarke turned to go, leaving his mostly untouched drink on the table.

"Roarke." His father followed him toward the door.

"Yes, sir?" Roarke turned to face him.

"What Angela said… Is it true about you and Currin's daughter?"

Roarke rubbed the back of his neck. "I like her. A lot. But I'm not really sure where things will go from here. I don't see the point in starting something when she's opening a new business here and I've got my practice in Dallas."

"True." Sterling nodded sagely. "But Houston is your home. It's where your family is. Your sisters and I would love it if you moved back."

"I appreciate the thought. But I'm happy in Dallas." Roarke patted his father's shoulder. "Good night."

He stepped outside and inhaled deeply, thankful for the fresh air that filled his lungs. The den had suddenly seemed like too small a space, the air dense and stale. He felt as if he could breathe easily for the first time since his father began his apology.

Roarke headed toward his rental, knowing there was only one person he wanted to call.

Fifteen

Annabel lifted a handful of scented bubbles and blew, watching as they scattered. She was an adult and yet she loved a good bubble bath as much as she had as a young child. She'd even vlogged from her tub about the use of various DIY skin care treatments. Wearing a bikini, of course. But tonight, she was just relaxing after a long day at the shop. A day filled with both good news and bad.

Wonderful moments, like meeting the Lewistons and the incredible kiss she shared with Roarke. However, there was the news that had hit her like a punch to the gut. She'd been a gullible fool where Mason was concerned. Then there was the argument with her brother over Roarke being her lawyer. And she couldn't help feeling slighted at Roarke's failure to acknowledge to her brother that they were more than just attorney and client.

Though, honestly, she couldn't exactly explain what their relationship was.

She knew that she wanted Roarke Perry in a way that had surprised her. And despite his reluctance, he seemed to feel the same.

Annabel extended one leg and slathered on her favorite DIY exfoliating mango sugar scrub.

She'd just climbed out of the tub and dried herself off when her phone rang. She secured the towel around her and answered it.

"Roarke. Hi."

"Hi, Annabel." He'd only spoken two words, but something in his voice alarmed her.

"Is everything okay?"

Roarke brought her up to speed on his father's case, including the news that they expected him to be released from house arrest soon.

"That's fantastic news, right?" She would've expected him to sound more excited about the fraud charges being dropped against Sterling.

"Yes," he agreed. "It's great news."

So why didn't he seem more excited about it?

There was something he wasn't saying.

"So why aren't you knocking back a couple of beers with your father right now?" she asked as she dried her hair.

"Sterling Perry is more of a single-malt whiskey kind of guy." There was humor in his voice, but there was still sadness there, too. "I just left the ranch, actually, and…" The line suddenly went quiet. She'd begun to wonder if she'd dropped the call when he finally spoke again. "You know, it's late. You're probably busy."

"Roarke, what is it?" Annabel sat on the edge of the tub. "Talk to me."

He hesitated before he spoke again. "Angela showed Sterling the results from the paternity test tonight. He wanted to talk about them."

"Is he questioning their validity?" She'd never been a fan of Sterling Perry. But if he'd caused Roarke even more pain, she might seriously reconsider her promise not to key anyone's car.

"No. He actually apologized." Roarke sounded as if he couldn't believe it. "He claims that it wasn't his intention to treat me poorly, but he admitted that his suspicion that I wasn't his biological son played an underlying role in our relationship."

She could feel his pain. Could hear the sadness, hurt and restrained anger beneath his reserved tone. And she had an overwhelming desire to comfort him.

"Hearing him finally apologize after all this time must've stirred up a lot of emotions for you. I can't begin to imagine what you're feeling, Roarke, but I'm here, if you need to talk."

"Sterling asked me to stay at the ranch tonight so we could watch old cowboy movies the way we did when I was a kid. It was…a nice gesture. Part of me appreciated the offer."

"But another part of you is finding it really hard

to just forgive and forget, as if none of this ever happened." Her heart broke for him.

"Precisely. It feels like I'm letting him off too easy." His voice was faint and sad. "Some part of me feels like he should suffer the way I did. I know that sounds awful. That I should just accept the olive branch he's extending."

She couldn't even begin to imagine the pain of having such a fractured relationship with a parent.

She'd often felt sorry for herself because at the age of ten she'd lost her mother to a cruel, insidious disease. She'd been acutely aware of her loss as she'd been planning her wedding. The moments that other brides-to-be cherished regularly brought her to tears.

But in listening to Roarke and feeling the deep-seated pain that had shattered his relationship with his father, she realized how lucky she'd been to have been born to Ryder and Elinah Currin. They'd made her feel abundantly loved and truly cherished.

"What you're feeling is human, Roarke. You've built a wall around your heart where your father is concerned. It was your way of dealing with the pain. It's not surprising that it would take some time for you to take that wall down."

"Thank you, Annabel."

"For what?"

"For understanding," he said simply. "I was listening to my father, trying to absorb what he was saying without drowning in this deluge of rage I've been tamping down my entire life. Suddenly, the night you and I went for a walk on the beach in Galveston popped in my head, and I knew I needed to talk to you. In fact, I wish we were there now."

"If you'd asked me to come to the beach with you tonight, Roarke, I would've said yes."

"Good to know." He seemed relieved. "Next weekend, maybe?"

"Maybe," she said. "But in the meantime, how about dinner at your place tomorrow? I'll bring the meal. I just need an address."

She typed the information into her phone and wished Roarke a good-night.

Annabel couldn't explain the strong pull she felt toward Roarke. Nor could she explain why they had clicked so instantly. She only knew that there was something special about the relationship they were building. And she couldn't bear to think of how much she'd miss him once he returned to his life in Dallas.

Roarke returned to his condo and tossed the keys onto the kitchen counter. His mind still buzzed with all the events of the day. He often worked late into the night when he was in the midst of a case. Yet, tonight his mind had reached the point of exhaustion.

He pulled a bottle of water out of the refrigerator and twisted off the cap.

Sterling Perry actually apologized.

Roarke was still in a partial state of shock, wondering if he'd dreamt it. He couldn't remember his father ever saying the word *sorry*. And he'd long given up imagining that his father would ever show any remorse about the way he'd treated him.

Sterling bought into the old-school mentality that apologizing was a weakness to be avoided at all costs. It was a philosophy Roarke didn't subscribe to.

In fact, he found it impossible to respect a person who lacked the courage or self-awareness to admit when they were wrong.

Seeing his father looking frail and humble had unnerved him. It was a running joke among his siblings that their father would probably outlive all of them because he was too ornery to ever die. But the man Roarke had seen tonight was a mere mortal in search of redemption.

Roarke stripped out of his clothing and hopped in the shower, hoping the hot water beating on his skin would help clear the muddled mess in his brain. Steam rose, filling the room as he lathered his body and washed his hair, his thoughts turning to Annabel.

His father had asked if he was serious about her. It was such a loaded question. One he didn't have a clear answer to.

He hadn't known Annabel Currin long. So why did it feel like he'd known her forever? And how was it that she seemed to know him in ways no one else did? Certainly not his family nor any woman he'd dated.

Annabel was playful and sweet. She brought out a side of him that he'd nearly forgotten about. And she reminded him that even when chaos swirled around him, it was okay to be human. To enjoy life and try to find happiness. Something he seemed to have forgotten in the years since he'd opened his practice.

Roarke loved his work and he took pride in helping others. But the cases he handled could be intense. He'd promised himself that he would never put business above family, the way his father had. Yet, before he'd returned home to help his father and met Annabel, his work had become the totality of his existence.

He couldn't remember the last time he'd truly enjoyed a meal prior to the breakfast Annabel had prepared at the beach. Back home, most of his meals consisted of the same boring takeout eaten mindlessly in front of a computer screen.

And it'd been ages since he'd done something as simple and magnificent as walking along the beach on a quiet night, as he'd done hand in hand with Annabel.

He knew all of the reasons he shouldn't be thinking of her the way he had been. He'd remembered them by rote. *Client. Family. Distance. Rebound.* He repeated them to himself as he lay staring at the ceiling, unable to sleep at night because thoughts of Annabel filled his head.

Roarke turned off the water and dried himself off with a thick bath towel. His skin still partially damp, he slipped on a faded T-shirt and an old pair of shorts to sleep in. Leftover college clothing he'd retrieved from his old bedroom at his father's ranch.

He went to the kitchen and searched through the fridge for a late-night snack before bed.

There was a knock at his door.

He checked his watch. It was just after midnight. It was undoubtedly his sister checking up on him after her date with Ryder to see how the conversation with their father had gone.

He considered not answering. After all, a part of him was still annoyed that his sister had forced the awkward conversation between him and Sterling.

There was another knock at the door, this one more persistent.

Roarke opened the door. "Look, Angela—"

"Guess again." Annabel wore an impish smile, her brown eyes filled with mischief. She held up two white paper bags. The savory, tantalizing aroma of its contents made his stomach rumble in anticipation. "I hope you aren't too disappointed. May I come in?"

"Of course." He stepped aside to let her in.

"It is officially tomorrow. So I'm here with dinner, as promised. It seemed like you needed a friend tonight."

"I must've sounded really pitiful on the phone." He kissed her cheek and relieved her of the bags. Its contents were still warm. "But I'm grateful you came. Now, what've you got?"

"I hope you're in the mood for Chinese. I wasn't sure what you'd like, so I got a little of everything. Ham-fried rice, chicken moo goo gai pan, pepper steak, pot stickers and egg rolls. They have the most authentic Chinese food in town. The neighborhood is a tad sketch and the late-night crowd can be sort of odd, but the food is *totally* worth it."

"I can't believe you risked life and limb to bring me takeout."

"You say that like it's crazy right now, but once you've tasted the food, it'll all make sense." She removed her leather backpack and set it on a chair. Her eyes scanned the space. "Nice condo."

"Thanks. Have a seat." He indicated the barstools in the kitchen. "I'll grab some plates, as soon as I figure out where they are." He opened one cabinet after another.

It'd been a long time since he'd stayed at the condo.

Annabel hopped off the stool and slid past him. "It might be quicker if I handle this."

He was inclined to argue, but she navigated the kitchen better instinctually than he had relying on his limited memory of the space.

She'd waved him off, indicating that he could sit down while she looked through the cupboards. But as he stood behind her, he was drawn to the heavenly sweet scent drifting from her golden brown skin.

He shut his eyes and repeated the words that were so familiar to him.

Client. Family. Distance. Rebound. Client. Family. Distance...

Roarke cursed under his breath as he opened his eyes, his gaze roaming over the flirty, white boho shift dress with a floral navy design. The hemline grazed her midthigh and the gauzy white fabric was slightly sheer, revealing the fitted lining beneath it that clung to her lean, shapely curves in all the right places.

His body tensed as the very last thread of his carefully-cultivated self-control snapped.

He stepped closer, his arms encircling Annabel's

narrow waist and nestling her firm round bottom tight against him, eliciting a soft gasp from her.

She rested her hands gently atop his. Her head lolled to one side and he took the opportunity to nuzzle her neck and inhale more of her enticing scent.

"God, you smell amazing, Annabel," he whispered against her skin. "Good enough to eat."

Her body melted against his and her chest rose and fell with increasingly shallow breaths. She swiveled her hips, increasing the contact between them.

He groaned in her ear in response to the delightful sensation of her curvy bottom grinding against him. He grew harder and his heart beat faster.

Roarke ran his tongue down the column of her graceful neck. Kissed the space where her neck and shoulder met.

Annabel responded with a soft purr as she looped one arm around his neck.

He kissed her shoulder, exposed by the neckline of her dress.

Roarke tugged the neckline down, exposing more of her silky skin. He trailed soft slow kisses along her shoulder and back as one hand glided up her stomach and cupped her firm breast, his palm teasing the stiff peak through the thin fabric.

His temperature rose and electricity zipped up his spine. He ached with desire for her. Roarke tugged the front of the dress down, exposing the round globe with its stiff brown peak. He grazed it with his thumb and she responded with a sensual murmur as she arched into his touch.

Roarke couldn't stand the anticipation another minute. He needed to taste her skin. To find out if it was as sweet as it smelled. He turned her toward him.

When she tipped her chin to meet his gaze, he was lost in her beautiful brown eyes. He leaned down, capturing her sensual lips in a greedy kiss.

He glided his hands down and gripped the hem of her dress, lifting over her head and tossing it onto a nearby barstool. Roarke lifted her in his arms and carried her to his bed.

The only meal he wanted now was Annabel Currin.

Annabel's heart raced and the damp space between her thighs throbbed like a steady heartbeat. Roarke laid her on her back in his bed and crawled on the mattress, hovering over her.

His woodsy, freshly scrubbed scent filled her nostrils and made her wonder about the taste of his skin.

He stripped off his faded college T-shirt and shorts, freeing his erection. Annabel sank her teeth into her lower lip. The pulsing of her core grew stronger.

The scruff on his chin grazed her skin as he laid kisses on her chest. When he took one of the sensitive nubs in his mouth and sucked it, she glided her fingers into his hair with a soft sigh.

He kissed his way down her body, smiling when he noticed the rose gold chains decorated with little charms across her hips between the sheer black panels of her floral lace bikini.

"Cute," he murmured against her skin, regarding the charms in the shapes of cherries, the letter x and a pair of red lips. "My favorite part is how easy it is to remove."

He unhooked the chains on either hip and kissed his way along the freshly shaven skin. Each kiss brought him closer to the space between her thighs, throbbing in anticipation of his touch.

When he pressed a kiss to her slick, swollen clit, she whimpered, her fingers gripping his short hair. When he laved it with his tongue, then sucked, she was sure she would explode. She dug her heels in the mattress as she moved against his mouth. Desperate for more of the delicious sensation.

Roarke spread her with his thumbs, his tongue stroking her sensitive flesh until she cried out with pleasure, her body trembling.

He crawled back up the bed, pressing a kiss to her ear. "You taste good everywhere," he whispered, his lips brushing her ear.

"I'm glad you approve." She panted, still trying to catch her breath.

He reached into the bedside table and pulled out an unopened box. Tearing into it, he removed a few of the little foil packets. Ripping one open, he sheathed himself before kissing her neck and moving on top of her.

Her body vibrated with need as Roarke pressed himself to her entrance, his gaze locked with hers. Annabel dug her fingers into his lower back, whimpering in response to the intense sensation of Roarke filling her as they moved together. She wrapped her legs around him, pulling him in deeper.

The friction of their bodies moving together brought her closer to the edge, her pleasure building until she cried out his name. Her body quivered and the space between her thighs pulsed.

He moved inside her, his breathing heavier, until his body went stiff and he found his release, his gaze meeting hers and her name on his lips.

The pulsing of his body inside hers sent ripples of pleasure through her, intensifying the incredible orgasm he'd already given her.

Roarke pressed a kiss to her lips, his thumb stroking her cheek. "You are absolutely incredible, Annabel."

He lay on his back and propped an arm behind his head.

"Hmm…" Annabel murmured dreamily as she nestled against him, her body thoroughly satisfied. She slung one arm across his waist and pressed a kiss to his chest. "And so are you."

But even as her body pulsed with intense satisfaction and her heart swelled with a growing affection for him, she couldn't stop thinking about how much it would hurt when it was time to let Roarke go.

Sixteen

Roarke's eyes slowly opened. The room was pitch-black, courtesy of the heavy room-darkening curtains that most executives seemed to prefer. He flipped his wrist and checked his watch. He'd ignored his earlier alarm and it was now nearly eight in the morning. Way past the time he usually awoke.

He stretched his free arm. The other was beneath Annabel as he cradled her to his chest.

He could become accustomed to waking up with Annabel in his arms.

They'd made love twice, then awakened in the middle of the night, eaten Chinese food in bed and then made love again.

It was no wonder they were both exhausted.

Roarke pressed a kiss to Annabel's forehead and

she muttered something before rolling over in the opposite direction.

Annabel Currin was everything he'd ever wanted in a woman. She was gorgeous, genuinely thoughtful, and she'd made him laugh so much his abdominal muscles were sore.

They'd been acquainted for such a short time. Yet, he'd developed such a deep affection for her. Feelings that seemed very much like love.

He let out a low groan and slid his arm from beneath Annabel before rolling out of bed. Roarke tossed out a few of the take-out boxes before stepping into the shower.

Hands pressed to the wall, he shut his eyes and let the warm water sluice over his skin.

Annabel.

She was a remarkable woman, unlike anyone he'd ever known. If the circumstances were different, he'd tell Annabel how he felt about her. But he wasn't interested in a long-distance relationship. And relocation wasn't an option for either of them.

So where did that leave them?

Completely screwed.

After their night at the beach, there was a part of him that wondered if he wouldn't have been better off if they'd never met. Then they wouldn't have to deal with the pain of saying goodbye. But he'd quickly realized that spending time with Annabel was a gift.

One he could never bring himself to regret.

The shower door opened, and he turned to see Annabel step inside. She wrapped her arms around him from behind, the side of her face pressed to his back.

"Good morning, handsome." She pressed a kiss to his damp skin. "How are you this morning?"

"Better now." He laid his hands atop hers and turned over one shoulder to kiss her. "I don't want you to think that this is the reason I called you last night. But I'm glad you came here, just the same."

"Good. Because I'm glad I came, too. In fact, I hope to do it again."

She kissed his back, her hand moving to stroke the erection, which had started the moment he'd laid eyes on her naked body stepping inside the shower.

He would've laughed at her pun, but his brain was too focused on the movement of her hand as she stroked his shaft slowly and deliberately, her naked breasts pressed into his back.

"Damn," he muttered beneath his breath. The sensation built, slowly rolling up his spine. His need was spiraling out of control. Every muscle in his body tensed, craving release.

"Babe, no." He could barely utter the words. But he needed her to stop before it was too late. As incredible as her firm, insistent pumping of his shaft felt, he wanted to come buried deep inside her, her slick, sensual flesh gripping his as he took them both on a sensual ride.

But Annabel had no intention of handing over the reins of control. She trailed kisses across his back as one hand glided up and down his steely length and the other cupped him from below. He'd lost the will to resist as the combination of erotic sensations sent him hurtling over the edge in a violent climax. Her hands gently squeezing and twisting until he'd been bled dry.

Breathing heavily, he collapsed against the wall, his hands pressed to the shower tiles. When he'd finally recovered, he turned around and kissed her, cradling her face as his tongue met hers in an intensely passionate kiss.

It was pointless to deny it. He was in serious danger of falling head over heels in love with Annabel Currin.

Roarke sat beside Annabel at the kitchen island, working on his second Belgian waffle. He was beginning to understand why some of his old college friends had gotten thicker in the middle after getting married. At this rate, he'd be sporting a spare tire by the end of the month.

And he could think of few better ways to spend his mornings than watching her move about the condo wearing one of his T-shirts.

The morning news played quietly on the television in the background as they chatted over breakfast. She'd shown him the portfolio of possible candidates for her next Fairy Godmother makeover. Some had been nominated by followers of her vlog. Others she'd learned about through women's shelters and other local charities she often partnered with.

He hadn't realized that there was so much more to these women's stories than a desire for pretty clothing and expensive makeup. Some of the women were cancer survivors. A few had lost everything in a natural disaster. Others were rebuilding their lives after dealing with unspeakable hardships.

Suddenly, it became clear why he and Annabel had so much in common. Despite growing up surrounded by wealth, they were both driven to give back and do good in the world, each of them in their own way.

"It's always so hard to decide who gets awarded with a Fairy Godmother makeover each quarter. But with the income from the spa and the vintage consignment shop, I'll be able to give away a lot more makeovers to women who need help reentering the workforce."

"You're an amazing woman, Annabel." Roarke handed her cell phone back to her. "Mason Harrison wasn't even close to being good enough for you. I'm sorry for any pain he brought you, but you deserve so much better." He kissed her cheek.

"Like maybe a crusading young attorney who fights the good fight, not knowing if he'll ever be paid a dime for his work?" A sexy smile spread across her face. He wanted to glide his palms up her thighs, drag the scraps of lace down her legs and take her right there on the barstool.

"No." He leaned in and kissed her softly, then whispered in her ear. "You deserve much better than him, too."

A deep frown marred her beautiful face. Then she quickly changed the subject. "I'm eager to get started on the renovations for Fairy Godmother. I hope to have it open around the time that the Texas Cattle-man's Club building renovations are done. Maybe I'll be able to do some sort of collaboration with the club."

"Sounds like a good idea." He nodded. "I know you're eager to get the reno started and that you like Davis Lewiston and his grandson—"

"Elliot. He's going to be great on camera." She jotted down a few notes in the black leather-bound traveler's notebook where she kept track of future vlog ideas. "And yes, I really like them."

"Just don't get too attached before you see their estimate and check a few more of their references," he suggested. "I admire your passion for this project, but when it comes to business decisions, it's best to approach the situation logically rather than with your heart."

"I appreciate your concern, Roarke." She glanced at him briefly before returning her attention to the leather notebook inscribed with her name. "But you know I could never work with someone who doesn't get me, right?"

"Then I guess it's a good thing I do." Roarke leaned in to kiss the maple syrup from her pouty lips.

"I guess it is." Her smile barely curved her lips and was in direct contrast to the sadness in her eyes.

He stroked her cheek with his thumb. "What is it?"

"Nothing I want to think about right now." She put down her pen and shifted her attention to the television. Her eyes suddenly went wide as she pointed to the screen. "Isn't that your father?"

Roarke turned toward the television, then scrambled for the remote to turn up the sound.

Sterling was dressed in a suit and wearing a Stetson. He stood outside the Perry Holdings offices, holding a briefcase and responding to questions posed by a handful of reporters. The scrolling headline at the bottom of the screen proclaimed that the fraud charges had been dropped against Perry Holdings CEO, Sterling Perry. Reporters peppered his father with questions:

"Where's the money?"

"Who killed Vincent Hamm?"

"Dammit." Roarke dragged a hand across his forehead. Sterling's growing irritation with the reporters' rapid-fire, accusatory questions was evident in his body language and the hardening of his scowl.

"Do I look like the kind of man who needs to resort to murder to get things done?" his father seethed.

"That isn't a denial, Mr. Perry," a local investigative reporter pointed out. "Did you have anything to do with the death of your employee Vincent Hamm? My source suspects that he discovered fraud going on at the company and was killed before he could go public with the information."

"Then your source is a damn liar. Because those accusations are preposterous." His father's face was flushed. He pointed in the woman's face aggressively.

"Stop talking and go inside the building right now. She isn't the FBI. You don't have to answer her questions," Roarke yelled at the television. He realized that his father couldn't hear his armchair quarterback pleas, but he uttered them just the same.

Roarke picked up his cell phone and called Angela. The phone rang until the call rolled over to voice mail. He sent a text message to his father in all caps.

STOP TALKING TO REPORTERS NOW. BEFORE YOU TALK YOURSELF INTO A CIVIL SUIT OR A MURDER CHARGE.

"I've gotta get down there before his mouth gets him into an entirely new set of charges." Roarke turned to Annabel, who continued to watch the spectacle with wide eyes. "Stay as long as you'd like. But if you leave, you'll need a key to lock the door behind you."

Roarke rummaged in a drawer and produced a spare key, handing it to Annabel.

"I know you probably have a busy day planned, but I'd really love to see you later this evening." He kissed her again. "This time, dinner is on me."

He tucked her hair behind her ear, remembering how it had looked spread across his bare chest earlier that morning.

"I'll be here," Annabel said, the same sadness in her voice. "And I've been giving you the best Houston has to offer in fine-ish dining. I expect the same effort, sir."

Roarke chuckled. It alleviated the aggravation he was feeling about his father's impromptu press conference.

"You've got it. We can talk then."

He hurried into his bedroom and got dressed before returning to the kitchen, giving Annabel one more kiss and snagging an apple on his way out the door.

Annabel sat on the barstool in Roarke's kitchen, feeling more comfortable than she'd ever been at Mason's condo. They'd been engaged for nearly a year and she never earned an official drawer at his place.

That should've been her first clue Mason was trash.

Everything felt more open and different with Roarke.

Last night had been incredible and she'd loved waking up in his bed and joining him in the shower. She'd loved making breakfast for him and talking about their day and their respective businesses.

She enjoyed being with Roarke. But as soon as his father's case was over, he would return to Dallas. Then their time together would be over.

Unless I can find a way to keep him in Houston.

But her life and new business were here in Houston and his life and his law practice were in Dallas. It'd taken a family crisis and a paternity test to drag Roarke back home. Not even his sisters had been able to convince him to return to Houston.

So what hope did she have of convincing him to stay on the chance that what was happening between them had the potential to be genuine?

She paced the floor, wearing one of Roarke's T-shirts, her feet stuffed into his oversize slippers.

Annabel glanced at the television and smiled, an idea brewing in her head.

Perhaps there was a way to convince Roarke he could stay in Houston *and* keep doing the work he loved.

It was a risky plan, but it was her only chance of convincing Roarke to stay. And if she had any chance of making the plan work, she'd have to make a deal with the devil himself.

Seventeen

Ryder Currin was fully aware that his daughter was an adult who had every right to spend the night wherever she pleased. Still, it bothered him that she had been mysteriously spending nights with a *friend*. Out of his three children, Annabel had always been the one who was most open about her love life. So it was especially perturbing that she'd suddenly become cryptic about what she was doing and whom she was doing it with.

He certainly didn't need to know all the hairy details. But he wanted to know that his little girl was somewhere safe.

His earlier calls to his daughter had gone unanswered. He was about to try again when his executive assistant buzzed him to say that Annabel was there to see him.

"Annabel. Nice of you to show up before I sent the cavalry out to rescue you." Ryder frowned, his elbows on his desk.

"Don't be so melodramatic, Dad." She kissed his cheek before unceremoniously plopping onto the leather seat in front of his desk, the way she'd been doing since she was a kid. In some ways, very little had changed. "Besides, it's not like you were home, anyway. You were on another one of your hot dates with Angela."

"I know I'm a fairly laid-back guy, but let's not forget that I'm the father here." He pointed a finger.

"And let's not forget that I'm not twelve." She shook a finger and mimicked his voice.

He couldn't help laughing. Annabel had mastered turning the tables on him and her late mother. She made them laugh so hard they'd nearly forgotten why they were scolding her in the first place.

Still, Annabel was a good kid. And she was a smart, generous, giving adult whom he was proud to have as his daughter. So he'd often given her a little more latitude than he'd given his older son, Xander, or his younger daughter, Maya. Still, as always, Annabel was pushing the boundaries.

"Okay, Ms. Adult. Let's have an open, honest conversation about our love lives. I'll go first." He cleared his throat and for a moment, he felt a little green around the gills. "Last night I realized my relationship with Angela Perry... This isn't just a fling. We've gotten very serious. Annabel, I love her. I can see a future for us together."

"Wow." His daughter nodded pensively. "Have you talked to Xander or Maya?"

"No," he admitted. "You're the reasonable one, so I thought I'd float the whole thing past you first." When she didn't respond, he added, "I thought you liked Angela."

"I do. And I think you two are good together. I'm just surprised, that's all."

Her lukewarm reception wasn't the reaction he was hoping for.

"Well…" Ryder sat back in his chair and steepled his fingers. "I want to know exactly what's on your mind. Even if you think I don't want to hear it."

Annabel wanted to be happy for her father, and on the surface, she was. But her parents had shared such a special relationship. And a part of her couldn't help mourning the loss of it.

Her parents' relationship had by no means been perfect, but it'd been damn close. It was the kind of relationship she hoped to have someday. The kind she honestly believed was possible with Roarke.

Though she was happy for her father, it saddened her to think of him leaving her mother's memory behind.

"I honestly am happy for you, Dad. You're a great father and a genuinely good person. You deserve this, and I know things will work out between you and Angela because you don't do anything half-heartedly."

"Thank you, Annabel. Your blessing means a lot to both of us." He smiled gratefully. "Now, your turn. What's with all of the sudden secrecy? It isn't like you."

"I know, and I'm sorry about that." She walked over to the office windows and peered out of the four-story building at the surrounding tree line.

"So what is it that you don't want to tell me? Have you and Mason gotten back together? Is that where you've been spending these mystery nights?"

"God, no." She recoiled at the very thought. "Mason was a complete snake. I'm glad he's out of my life and gone from the company."

When she turned back to her father, he seemed genuinely worried. He walked over to where she stood. "If not Mason, then who? You just ended your engagement and a two-year relationship."

Annabel met her father's gaze. "Roarke Perry."

"I thought he was supposed to be your attorney." Her father raised an eyebrow.

"He is," she confirmed.

He dragged a hand through his dark blond hair. Lines spanned his forehead and his lips twisted in a deep frown. "Didn't you two just meet at the charity gala? The night you went to the beach with your *mystery friend*."

"Yes, but he was a perfect gentleman, and I slept in my own room. Not that I owe anyone an explanation either way," she quickly added.

"I've always trusted you to make your own decisions, but I have to be honest, I'm concerned Roarke is taking advantage of you. You just got out of a long-term relationship. You're vulnerable right now, sweetheart. Then your attorney makes a pass at you…" He shook his head and sat in one of the chairs by the windows. "Sounds shady to me, pumpkin."

"The truth is, he didn't pursue me. I'm the one who pursued him." Annabel sat across from her father, trying to hide her amusement that he was shocked by her confession.

"So this is a rebound relationship, then." Her father frowned. "Another reason to use caution. Those can get real ugly, real fast. One person is always more invested than the other. Someone inevitably gets hurt. And, Annabel, I don't want that someone to be you."

"I know this seems sudden. But I'm sure of my feelings for Roarke. I've never felt like this about anyone."

"Annabel…" Her father huffed, unconvinced. "It always feels that way when a relationship is new."

She moved to the chair beside her father and took his hand. "Dad, this isn't a silly infatuation. Roarke is amazing. He's bright, and he's funny. And sometimes he's way too serious because he genuinely wants to make the world a better place. And it isn't just something he's saying because it sounds cool. He rejected a much easier life and higher-profile jobs with impressive salaries because he's committed to what he's doing."

"Sounds a bit too good to be true, darling." His tone was apologetic.

"Because he's sweet and generous and kind? I happen to know for a fact that men like that exist. I was raised by one."

"I appreciate the compliment, sweetheart. But that doesn't change the fact that this is all happening too fast."

"Isn't that what your parents thought when you met Mom in Kenya and fell head over heels for her in just a few weeks?" Annabel met her father's skeptical gaze.

His mouth twisted in a sad smile. "Things were different for your mother and me. For one thing, she hadn't just broken up with a man she'd planned to marry in a few weeks." He gave her his best wise fatherly look.

"But you were both about the same age as Roarke and I are now. You two had a whirlwind affair and then decided to get married. Everyone in her village, including her parents, thought she was crazy to suddenly fall in love with and marry some Western man who lived on the other side of the world." Annabel recounted every bit of the tale of her parents' love affair. A story they had told her many times when she was a little girl. "And your friends and family thought you'd lost it for falling in love with a total stranger in Africa and bringing her here to Houston to make a life with her."

"Your mother never felt like a stranger. From the moment I laid eyes on her..." He shrugged. "There was something so familiar about her. And those mischievous dark eyes of hers... It was like they could see right through me. I swear, sometimes it felt like she knew what I was thinking before I did."

"Exactly." Annabel smiled, tears stinging her eyes. "But she never regretted that choice, Dad. Not even for a minute."

"Neither have I." He gave her a pained smile.

"I'm glad neither of you listened to your well-meaning friends and family. Because they turned out to be terribly wrong."

"Okay, Annabel." He squeezed her hand. "You've made your point. A little time with a lawyer and you're starting to sound like one."

Maybe she had learned a thing or two from Roarke.

"But what do you really know about this man? Angela always speaks of her brother in glowing terms, but she could easily have a blind spot where he's concerned. Besides, he's been living in Dallas for years. There could be a whole other side of him Angela knows nothing about."

"Roarke is a really good guy, Dad. If you spent even a little time with him, you'd recognize that."

"And whose fault is it I haven't had that opportunity?" He narrowed his gaze and released her hand.

"I know, I know. But the relationship between us is complicated. To be honest, neither of us has admitted that we're actually in a relationship."

"So you two are just hooking up, then?" Ryder's gaze hardened. "What happens when he's finally gotten Daddy Warbucks off and he hops a 747 for Dallas again? Where will that leave this relationship that's not a relationship?"

"That's why I'm here. I have an idea that would resolve our long-distance problem."

Her father sat back in the chair and crossed one ankle over his knee, his hands clasped over his abdomen. "I've got a feeling I'm gonna regret saying this, Annabel, but tell me about it."

Eighteen

Roarke had gotten up early and retreated to his office to prepare an amicus brief for the Texas Supreme
Court on behalf of a small nonprofit organization he
represented.

The organization was filing a civil suit against a
company that had defrauded them. However, another
agency's criminal case against the organization had
gone all the way to the state supreme court. So the
nonprofit had been invited to file a friend-of-the-court
brief to provide the deciding judges with a more sweep-
ing view of the issue before them.

A sudden smile broke across his face as he remembered that Annabel was still lying in his bed naked,
her hair wrapped in a colorful silk scarf.

For the past week, Annabel had spent most nights

in his bed. Waking up to her sweet face and lush curves was a luxury he'd come to treasure.

They'd spent their evenings cooking together or watching television. Sometimes they worked together in companionable silence in his office. It was a life he could easily imagine settling into.

But they'd spent the past week actively avoiding the talk they both knew they needed to have.

What would happen when his stay in Houston came to an end?

It was something, it seemed, that neither of them wanted to consider.

Roarke's thoughts were interrupted by an email alert from Mason Harrison. It shouldn't have surprised him that an arrogant bastard like Mason Harrison would wait until the very last day to reply to their demand that he repay Annabel and her family in full for everything they'd lost in the planning of their wedding.

Roarke had expected to hear from the man's lawyer, requesting to negotiate the amount. Instead, the reply came directly from Mason. He agreed to compensate Annabel for the full amount under one condition. That he got to make his apology to her in person.

Roarke rubbed his whiskered chin. He didn't like it. Why wouldn't a man as savvy as Mason hire a lawyer? Why wouldn't he negotiate the terms? And what was with the personal apology?

Roarke minimized the email. He'd discuss it with Annabel when she awoke.

He returned to writing the amicus brief, thankful

that the past week had been relatively calm. There hadn't been any new bombshells regarding the dropped fraud charges against his father or the still-open investigation of Vincent Hamm's murder. But rather than being encouraged by it, Roarke felt sure it was the eye of the storm. They were being lulled into a false sense of calm.

Perhaps by design.

The sound of the shower running pulled him from his thoughts. Since that morning in the shower together, it was the vision that played over and over again in his mind whenever he heard the water running. For a moment, he contemplated joining her.

His cell phone rang and he answered. "Good morning, Dad," Roarke greeted his father. Thankfully, they'd come to an agreement that he'd stop running his yap to reporters and practice the simple art of stating *No comment* or *Please refer all questions to my lawyers*.

So far, so good. Maybe there was hope for Sterling Perry after all.

"Good morning, son." Sterling sounded hesitant. He cleared his throat. "I'm calling you with a proposal."

"What kind of proposal?" Roarke sat back in his chair.

Sterling cleared his throat again. Another sign that there was something suspicious about his father's request, whatever it might be.

"You know that we're opening a chapter of the Texas Cattleman's Club here in Houston?"

"Yes. What of it?"

"I have a twofold request. First, I'd like you to join the club. I'll sponsor your membership, of course."

"Why would you do that? Besides, I live in Dallas. If I was going to join the club, why wouldn't I join there?"

"Because of the second part of the proposal. Now, just hear me out before you go turning it down."

Roarke dragged a hand through his hair and nodded. "Okay. Let's hear the rest."

"As part of the club's outreach to the community, I'd like to start a legal fund for those who can't afford representation. But rather than hiring random lawyers who may or may not be very good, we would use the fund to pay an annual salary of a single lawyer. *You*."

"You want me to become some sort of outreach lawyer at the club?" The proposal didn't sound like anything his father might have thought of. So where was the request coming from? "Besides, I thought the new president of the club hadn't been named. I doubt that Ryder Currin would go along with such a plan, should he be named president."

"Actually, this is a plan that we've both agreed to, regardless of which one of us becomes president."

"You talked to Ryder about this?"

"Indirectly." His father was being squirrelly with his answers.

The water in the shower stopped running, drawing his attention to the source of the sound. Suddenly, his father's odd venture into humanitarianism made sense.

"Let me guess, you had a talk with his daughter Annabel. She's the brainchild behind this plan to what…bring me back to Houston?"

Sterling didn't answer right away. "It's what you enjoy doing, Roarke. Does it matter where you practice law as long as you get to help the people who need it? I assure you, there are just as many clients in need of your services here as there are in Dallas. Perhaps more."

"It matters if the three of you are conspiring behind my back to make it happen. Not a single one of you thought that maybe you should ask if I have any interest in returning to Houston?"

"Annabel certainly seems convinced," Sterling said. "And for the record, son, I like her. Seems to me that a man would be pretty damn lucky to have a woman go to this kind of trouble on his behalf."

"You don't get it, do you, Dad? No one wants to be manipulated. Not even if the person doing it has the purest intentions."

"Roarke—"

"I don't need your charity, *Sterling*. If I ever choose to return to Houston, it'll be on my own terms. Not because the three of you thought it would be fun to play puppet master."

"Then there's another option I'd urge you to consider, son. I'd like you to rethink coming to work for Perry Holdings. I know the company has taken a hit. But the fraud charges have been dropped and we've been working the PR angle. It's only a matter of time before the company's valuation rises again."

"We've been through this before, Dad. I'm not interested in working for Perry Holdings. Not as long as you treat rules and ethics as an inconvenient suggestion."

"I thought after the talk we had at the ranch that you and I would get a fresh start."

"I want that, too. But that doesn't change the fact that we have diametrically opposed business philosophies."

"If you believe that things should be cleaned up at Perry Holdings, who better to do it than a man with high character and a vested interest in this family's legacy?"

Roarke didn't respond. Was Sterling actually offering him carte blanche to ensure everything at the company was aboveboard?

He rubbed at the tension building in his temple. "I have to go, Dad. We'll talk later."

He ended the call. Roarke's pulse raced and the band of tension tightened around his head, as if it were trapped in a vise.

It was time that he and Annabel talk.

Annabel knocked lightly on the partially closed door to Roarke's office. She'd spent most evenings at his condo over the past week. Yet, she tried to be respectful of his privacy, especially when he was working.

There was no answer.

She tapped lightly again. She didn't want to disturb Roarke in the event that he was dictating notes to his assistant, Marietta, back in Dallas.

"Come in." Roarke's voice was strained. Nothing like the playful, sexy tone with which he greeted her most mornings.

Annabel approached Roarke with a tentative smile, hoping that there hadn't been more bad news in the pending murder case or in one of his client's cases.

She slid onto his lap, as she often did, and pressed a kiss to his mouth.

He allowed her to kiss him, but he didn't kiss her back. Nor did he wrap his arms around her the way he usually did.

Something is very wrong.

"I need to put my attorney–client hat on. So if you wouldn't mind?" He motioned for her to take the guest chair on the other side of the desk.

She complied, smoothing her skirt. "Okay, what's this about? Did Mason finally reply to our letter?"

"He did. Surprisingly, he's agreed to compensate you for all monies lost. Including the wedding dress." Roarke moved his mouse, presumably opening Mason's email.

"That is surprising, but that's good news, isn't it?" They should be celebrating, preferably in bed. Or the shower. Or the sofa. Or…

"It is good news. I'm just reluctant to take Harrison's offer at face value. Especially since he's making it contingent upon providing you with a full apology in person."

"Why doesn't he just pick up the phone? Or email? Send a text even? I don't need to see him."

Roarke was slow to respond. "Are you afraid that if you do see him… Do you still have feelings for him, Annabel?"

"I do. But none that I can articulate without filling an entire cuss jar." She shifted in her chair and tugged her hair over one shoulder. "When and where does he want to meet?"

"He didn't indicate either in his email. So don't be surprised if he contacts you directly to work out a time and place. If you're uncomfortable negotiating the terms—"

"No, I'm not." She shrugged. "He's a jerk, but he's not dangerous." She sat forward. "You seem stressed. Bad news on one of your other cases?"

"No." His brows furrowed in an expression that looked very much like disappointment. "But I did get some disturbing news this morning."

"What's wrong? Is your family okay?" Now she was worried, too.

"I spoke with my father this morning. It seems he and Ryder have decided that the Houston chapter of the Texas Cattleman's Club should have an ongoing outreach program to provide legal aid." He watched her carefully.

"That's sounds like a terrific program. And it's an excellent fit for you, Roarke." Annabel smiled tentatively. He didn't seem excited or even surprised by the news from his father. Instead, he regarded her suspiciously.

"It is, Annabel. Almost as if it was tailor-made for me." He rubbed his chin as he assessed her. His glare had the effect of hot lights in an interrogation room. She could only imagine how intimidating he must be in the courtroom.

"So what if it was tailored for you, Roarke?" Annabel asked, her eyes searching his. "It's still a much-needed program here in Houston. And can you think of a better person to run it?"

"Except I already have my own practice doing just that in Dallas." Roarke's cheeks were flushed and his eyes were the color of a stormy sea. He stood, his hands pressed to the desk as he leaned forward. "So what would possibly give my father or yours the idea that I'm interested in trading my practice in Dallas for one here?"

His words hit her with the impact of a two-ton wrecking ball.

Annabel's eyes stung with tears and a knot tightened in her belly. The first time Roarke had really kissed her, she felt a shock of electricity and a fluttering in her chest. She'd known, in that instant, how deeply she'd been attracted to him. That she didn't just want some casual fling with him.

She'd been falling for Roarke little by little, since their first encounter. The night they'd made love for the first time, she thought he felt the same.

But as he assessed her now with his chilly stare, none of the affection she'd been so sure he felt for her was evident.

"You've obviously already determined that this

was my idea. I just thought that with everything that's happened between us and with your family…" Annabel's courage withered beneath Roarke's unyielding glare. She blinked back the tears that threatened to fall, her gaze not meeting his.

"You didn't even bother to ask me, Annabel. Instead, you went behind my back and talked to your father and mine. You know my history with Sterling. That he's been trying to manipulate me my entire life." Roarke's voice was strained.

"It's not like your father came up with a plan to make you do something you don't want to do, Roarke."

"No, he didn't. *You did.*" He pointed an accusatory finger in her direction. "You actually managed to flip the script on Sterling. Got him to do *your* bidding. If I wasn't so pissed right now, I might actually be impressed."

Annabel's cheeks burned beneath his stare, a mixture of anger and disappointment. She'd realized she was taking a risk with this plan. But she hoped Roarke would see it as proof of just how much he meant to her.

"I'm sorry. I obviously misread the situation."

"Look, Annabel, I've been honest with you from the beginning about all of the obstacles we faced. I thought you'd accepted that."

"You're right. You were adamant that we should never have gotten involved. I'm the one who pursued you. And I'm the one who made the mistake of thinking that maybe you had reason to come home." Her voice quivered slightly.

"Dallas *is* my home, Annabel." He narrowed his gaze at her. "And I've never made you believe otherwise."

A fresh round of tears stung her eyes. "But that isn't the problem, is it? You're afraid."

"And what is it you think I'm afraid of?" He tipped his chin.

"*This*. Us. You're afraid of how you feel. That this could be something real and worth making sacrifices for."

"You shouldn't have gone to my father behind my back. All you had to do was roll over in bed and ask me what I wanted."

"I've tried. You always change the subject." Her eyes stung and her throat felt dry and tight. "I guess that was my answer all along. I just didn't expect to fall in love with you."

Annabel stood, drawing in a shaky breath. "And for the record, I'm scared, too. But I'd rather take a risk than miss out on something incredible because I was too afraid to try. Wouldn't you?"

She stared at him through watery eyes.

"I can't do this right now." He shifted his gaze from hers and returned to his chair. "I only have forty-eight hours to put together an important court brief. I can't afford any distractions. Happy or otherwise."

He'd used the phrase she'd uttered the night they

had drove out to Galveston. When she'd said that meeting him had been a happy distraction.

That night seemed like a lifetime ago.

"So then nothing has changed for you? That's all we are? Just a distraction from everything else going on in our lives?" She swallowed back tears and the hurt pride that squeezed her chest. "Well, don't let me distract you any further."

Annabel slipped out of Roarke's office and gathered her things, leaving his spare key on the counter. She got on the elevator and made her way down to the garage.

She'd told Roarke she was in love with him and he hadn't even acknowledged her words.

Her heart ached and hot tears ran down her cheeks. But it was better to find out now that she'd been wrong about Roarke.

He could never love her the way she already loved him.

Nineteen

Angela strolled hand in hand with Ryder after a night of seeing *Hamilton* on tour at Sarofim Hall at the Hobby Center. It was a beautiful night, so they walked the half mile to Spindletop, a revolving glass-walled restaurant that provided 360-degree views of the city, for a lovely meal.

Ryder looked particularly handsome tonight. He'd ditched his customary dark brown Stetson and had allowed his dark blond hair to grow out a little longer because she loved running her fingers through it.

Ryder wasn't a fan of suits, but he looked handsome in a gray vest, crisp white shirt with French cuffs and a black tie with gray and white diagonal stripes.

Ryder ran his fingers through his hair, flipping back a few strands that had fallen across his eye.

After they'd finished their meal, he reached across the table and took her hands in his.

"I know I've already told you this, but you look stunning in that blue dress." He squeezed her hands. "It's been such a perfect night."

"It has," she agreed. "The show was fabulous. The food was delicious. And the company was outstanding. I couldn't imagine a more perfect night."

"I don't know about that. The night's not over." He winked. "I ordered dessert."

"When?"

"When I stepped away from the table." He grinned.

"That's sweet of you." Angela placed a hand on her belly. It was already filled to capacity. They'd shared barbecue bourbon shrimp and smoked salmon carpaccio appetizers. Then they had an entrée of a seafood pot for two. "But I honestly don't think I can eat another bite."

"Good thing I just got one slice to share." He released her hands and sat back as their server approached.

The woman practically beamed as she set the slice of cheesecake on the table, then walked away.

Angela glanced down at the dessert and noticed a brilliant shimmer coming from it.

What...

"Oh, my God, is that— I mean, are you—" Her heart raced and she couldn't get the words out.

"Yes and yes." He took her hands in his again,

bringing one to his mouth and kissing the back of it. "These past few months that we've spent together have been incredible. I didn't think I'd ever find love again. Nor was I looking for it. But you shook things up. Awakened this dormant heart. You made me believe that love was possible again." He grazed the back of her hand with his thumb. "Experience has taught me that when you find love, you shouldn't hesitate. You never know what tomorrow'll bring. And I don't want to miss out on another precious moment with you." He removed the ring from its perch atop the cheesecake. Its large-carat, round-cut center diamond and ribbons of pavé diamonds set in a platinum band gleamed. Then he got down on one knee before her. "Angela, darlin', will you marry me?"

"Yes. Of course, I will, Ryder." Angela nodded wildly, tears streaming down her face. "I had started to think my cowboy would never come along. But there you were. The man I'd been waiting for my whole life. You're everything I dreamed of and more. And I am so very much in-love with you."

Ryder slipped the ring on her finger. When she leaned down and kissed him, the nearby patrons and staff cheered and applauded.

She and Ryder Currin were going to get married.

Angela could barely contain her joy.

But how would their families react?

She only hoped that their families would be half as happy for them as the restaurant filled with strangers seemed to be.

* * *

It'd been two days since Annabel had walked out of Roarke's condo, and he hadn't called.

She'd overplayed her hand when she'd come up with her plan to get Roarke to move back to Houston. Her motive certainly hadn't been diabolical. She just wanted him in her life, there in Houston, surrounded by their families.

She hadn't realized that he'd have such a harsh reaction to her meddling.

So she'd thrown herself into her work and tried to pretend that it didn't feel as if the entire world had crashed down around her. She'd honestly felt a sense of relief when Mason had broken off their engagement. But with Roarke gone from her life, it felt as if she was missing an essential organ.

Her life just wasn't the same without him.

She stood in the center of the kitchen at their family ranch when sounds of laughter rung throughout the house. It was her father and Angela.

"Hey there, darlin'." Her father kissed her cheek as he entered the kitchen, still holding Angela's hand in his.

"Sounds like you two had a great night." She forced a smile. They'd gone to the theater and then out to dinner. The way the two of them were giggling, she was guessing they'd hit the wine particularly hard.

"It was amazing." Angela stared dreamily into her father's eyes. As much as Annabel liked the woman, there was a moment of envy that made her want to puke. Angela extended the hand that her father wasn't holding. "We got engaged!"

"You two are getting married? Wow, that's awesome." Fat tears burned Annabel's eyes and streamed down her cheeks. She forced a big smile as she hugged them both, joy and envy battling in her chest. "I'm really happy for the two of you."

"Thank you, Annabel." Angela squeezed her hand as she embraced her new fiancé. "Your support and acceptance right from the very beginning has meant so much to us."

More tears slid down Annabel's cheeks. She could only imagine the kind of pushback Angela had gotten about the relationship from Sterling and probably from her sisters and brother. But unlike Roarke, Angela had been willing to fight for what she wanted.

"I'm glad you were here. You've been spending so much time with Roarke, I didn't know if we'd get to tell you in person." Her father pulled a bottle of champagne out of the fridge.

"I'm glad I was here, too." Annabel forced an even bigger smile, determined not to rain on their parade. She hadn't told her father about the argument between her and Roarke. And she wouldn't let them know just how much her heart was breaking now.

"We should all go out to celebrate." Her father squeezed Angela's hand. "Once we tell Sterling, we should invite him, too. Whether or not he accepts is up to him."

Angela nodded, looking hopeful. "It's late. I'll tell my family tomorrow night."

"Are you sure you we shouldn't do this together? Maybe we should build a wall of solidarity right from the start, so Sterling won't think he can divide and conquer."

"No, I think I should talk to him alone first. But I promise, there will be no dividing and conquering. We're in this together." She pressed a quick kiss to his lips.

Annabel suddenly felt like a third wheel.

The ranch was large and her father's bedroom was in a different wing of the house from hers. Still, it felt as if she was encroaching on their big night.

"Maybe I should go and give you kids some space," Annabel teased.

"No, don't go." Angela grabbed her hand. "This is your home. I'm the intruder."

Annabel smiled. "You're not an intruder. You're family. Starting right now."

Ryder smiled to himself as he watched his beautiful fiancée sleeping in his king-size bed. His son, Xander, and his lovely fiancée, Frankie, had come over and joined them for a celebration toast. They were gone and it was late, but he couldn't sleep. Partly because of the excitement of the engagement. Partly because he felt guilty that he hadn't told his youngest daughter, Maya, yet. She'd spent the summer at a job in Cape Cod and was about to start her second year at school in Boston College. He missed her.

He sent her a quick text message.

Hey darlin'. You up? Got some news.

His phone rang almost instantly, and he stepped outside on the patio to take the call.

After their pleasantries, he jumped right in to the reason for his call.

"Engaged to a Perry? Wow, Dad. I can't believe it. You're actually marrying into that family."

"A few months ago, if anyone had predicted this, I'd have thought they were auditioning for a strait-jacket. Guess life really is stranger than fiction."

Maya suddenly got quiet and Ryder held his breath, waiting for his youngest daughter to ask the question she'd been asking more frequently lately.

"I hate that I'm not there with you all to celebrate," Maya said finally. "Sometimes, I feel so disconnected from everyone."

"It's just homesickness, sweetheart. That's all. You'll adjust, I promise. And know that even when you're away, my baby girl is always in my thoughts."

Maya sighed softly. "I know, Dad. And I love you."

"Something bothering you, buttercup?" Ryder asked. He realized he was giving Maya a pathway to the very topic he didn't want to discuss, but it broke his heart to hear her sounding so sad and alone.

"Tonight's not the time. I'll call you later. After your champagne buzz wears off."

Ryder chuckled. "Sounds good. 'Night, sweet-heart."

He ended the call and poured himself the last of the champagne. Ryder knew exactly what Maya had wanted to ask. She wanted to know who her biological parents were.

Off to college and no longer a little girl, Maya had become more persistent about learning the identity of her birth parents. But when he and his wife Elinah had adopted Maya a little more than eighteen years before, he'd assured the girl's grandfather that he would never reveal the identity of her biological family. It was a promise that had become much harder to keep now that Maya was officially an adult and as stubborn as her sister, Annabel.

Maybe Maya would learn the truth one day. But as long as it was dependent upon him, he would try to keep his promise to her grandfather.

Now that all three of his children knew his happy news, Ryder felt a sense of relief. He turned off the bedside lamp and crawled into bed with his bride-to-be.

Twenty

Annabel entered Farrah's and scanned the coffee shop for Elliot Lewiston. He wasn't there for their meeting yet, but she was fifteen minutes early.

"What can I get for you, hon?" the woman behind the counter asked in a thick Texas drawl.

Before she could respond, a deep voice wafted over her head. "Slice of lemon icebox pie and a large Sumatran blend."

She didn't need to turn around to know whom the authoritative voice belonged to.

What is he doing here?

The cashier shifted her gaze to Annabel to confirm that was what she wanted. She nodded and pulled out her credit card, but Roarke handed the woman his instead.

"You really don't need to do that."

"I want to. Please." His tone was soft and pleading.

Annabel thanked him, then moved to the other end of the counter to wait for her order. Roarke joined her there after he'd placed his own.

"So…your dad popped the question to my sister," Roarke said as they stood side by side, watching the baristas prepare their orders. "They're both good people. I'm happy for them."

"Me, too. It's good to see my dad happy and in love again." Annabel scrolled through the comments on her Instagram feed.

"How did your brother and sister take the news?" Roarke asked after a few awkward moments of silence.

"They're happy for them, too." She didn't look up. "What about your father and your sisters?"

"Melinda and Esme adjusted to the news well enough. My father… Well, he reacted pretty well for him. I was actually kind of proud of him," Roarke said. "Have you met with Mason yet?"

"No." She turned to face him fully. "He had a family emergency out of town. He says he'll contact me when he returns."

"That's well past the stated deadline. You should've informed me that Mason didn't keep his end of the bargain."

"It didn't really seem like you wanted to hear from me again." She shrugged.

"I'm still your lawyer, Annabel. I wouldn't let…" He huffed. She wasn't sure if he was frustrated with her or with himself. "It's still my job to protect your interests in this matter."

"Well, Mr. Attorney, consider yourself informed. You now know everything I do."

"And I'm still waiting for you to forward me your renovation contract."

"Look, Roarke, I know you have more pressing client work to handle. I can find another attorney, if that would be better for you." She slid her phone in the back pocket of her jeans, picked up her order and put a tip in the jar.

Roarke caught her elbow. "I'd feel better if I reviewed that contract. I've seen a lot of the loopholes that unscrupulous contractors try to jump through."

"Fine. As soon as I get it, I'll email it to you." She tugged her arm from his grip. "Thank you again for the pie and coffee."

Annabel slid into a booth at the far end of the café. Her hands trembled beneath the table.

It was the first time she'd seen or talked to Roarke since she'd walked out of his condo. She'd tried to act nonchalant about their casual encounter, but standing so close to him, she could barely breathe. When he touched her, she'd been reminded of the way it had felt to wake up in his arms.

"Annabel, I think we should talk." Roarke slid into the seat across from her, startling her. "I hate the way we left things the other day. I overreacted."

"I appreciate that." She gripped her coffee cup. "And I apologize again for meddling in your life. I overstepped. You had every right to be angry."

"Annabel!" Elliot approached with a broad smile on his face, his clipboard underneath his arm. "Sorry I'm running behind. There was an accident on the way here."

"No worries. I'm just glad you're okay." She smiled warmly at him. "Elliot Lewiston, this is my attorney, Roarke Perry. He'll be reviewing the contract once it's ready. Roarke Perry, this is Elliot Lewiston, one half of my contracting team."

He reached down and shook Roarke's hand. "Pleasure to meet you, Mr. Perry."

"Elliot and I have a meeting scheduled, so perhaps we can talk another time." She looked at Roarke pointedly.

"Of course. Keep me posted on the arrangements with Mason." He stood and buttoned his gray suit jacket.

Elliot slid onto the seat Roarke vacated and opened his laptop.

"Roarke!" She called to him as he walked away. He turned back to her expectantly, his eyes wide and hopeful. She lifted the white bag and paper cup he'd left behind. "Your pie and coffee."

"Oh, thank you." His voice was filled with disappointment. He came back to retrieve them. "Have a good meeting."

Annabel watched as he turned and walked out the door, her heart aching and her stomach tangled in knots. It'd taken every ounce of control she could muster to keep her expression neutral when she talked to Roarke. To behave as if running into him in her favorite coffee shop was no big deal, when it felt as if her heart was breaking all over again.

"Annabel, is everything okay?" Elliot asked. "If this isn't a good time for you—"

"Now is perfect, Elliot." Annabel forced a wide smile and rubbed her hands together eagerly. "I can't wait to see what you and Mr. Lewiston have for me."

"Actually, it'll be easier if I come on that side of the table." Elliot turned his open laptop toward Annabel and joined her on the other side of the booth.

Annabel shut her eyes momentarily and sighed quietly, determined to put all thoughts of Roarke Perry out of her mind long enough to focus on the future of Fairy Godmother.

Roarke returned to his rental SUV and slammed his fist on the steering wheel.

Annabel was right. He was a coward. He'd been afraid to admit his feelings for her, even to himself. Afraid to consider that there actually might be something to this whole idea of their being meant to be together. Because since she'd walked out his front door, he felt as if his entire world had grown dark and cold.

Until a few weeks ago, he'd lived a simple, solitary, focused life. One devoid of family or romantic entanglements. But he was doing a tremendous amount of good in the world, and he'd been content with his life.

But then Annabel Currin had smiled at him in that damned coffee shop and it had turned his entire world upside down. She'd reminded him that he could do good in the world *and* be happy. And that just because his parents' love story wasn't a happy one, it didn't mean that he was doomed to experience their fate.

Roarke had always considered himself to be sensible and clearheaded. He had lofty ideals, which had prevented him from working with his father at Perry Holdings. Yet, he was quite practical about the realities of the way the world worked.

None of that prepared him for the possibility of meeting the woman who felt like "the one" and falling in love so quickly. The realist in him had refused to believe it was possible. But the hole that had been left in his heart when he let her walk away made the depth of his feelings for her quite real.

His heart and his home felt empty without her.

He'd missed Annabel from the moment she'd left his condo. But he'd been too proud and stubborn to go after her or pick up the phone and call. So maybe there was more of Sterling Perry in him than he cared to admit.

Instead, he'd gone to her favorite coffee shop twice a day, hoping their paths would cross so they could talk on neutral ground. Her meeting with Elliot Lewiston had thrown him off, and he'd lost his nerve. But he wouldn't let her walk away again. Not without laying his heart on the line and telling her the truth.

Because Annabel Currin was worth the risk.

Twenty-One

Annabel got out of her car at the future site of her business and popped the trunk. After her meeting at the coffee shop with Elliot Lewiston she'd gone to a home improvement warehouse to look at paints. She picked up a slew of sample paints within the three different color schemes the designer had proposed. Now she had to decide which one would look best in the space.

She slid her phone into her back pocket and reached for the box of paint samples and brushes in her trunk.

"Let me help you with that."

She turned at the sound of his voice. "Are you stalking me now, Perry?" The sound of his smooth voice still did things to her body. No matter how much she wanted to pretend otherwise. "Wouldn't have pegged you for the stalker type."

"I assure you that I'm not. But I do really need to talk to you." Roarke lifted the cardboard box from the trunk.

"What is there to talk about?" Annabel picked up a few plastic bags filled with additional items she'd purchased for her office and the upstairs bathroom at the shop. She slammed the trunk and headed toward the side door of the building. "You made your feelings…or lack thereof…quite clear."

"Like I said, I overreacted. All I could think of was the many times my father has tried to manipulate me. Maybe I freaked out a little."

She glanced up at him. His tortured expression and the pain in his eyes tugged at her heart. She unlocked the door of the shop and stepped inside without responding.

"Where do you want this?" Roarke raised the box slightly as he glanced around the space.

"All of this is going upstairs in my office."

He held out the box, indicating that she should put her bags inside it, too. "Anywhere in particular?"

She handed over her bags. "On the floor in the corner is fine. I'll be up shortly. I just need to grab the mail first."

He nodded. "Then I hope we can talk, because I've been having this conversation in my head for the last few days and I'm eager to get it off my chest."

A knot tightened in Annabel's stomach. Roarke's need to talk could go either way. Was he willing to take a chance on them, even if they had to compromise and try a long-distance relationship first? Or did he want to make a clean break and walk away?

"Sure." The sound of her heartbeat filled her ears. "I'd like that."

She sucked in a deep breath, then slowly released it, as she went to retrieve the mail that had been dropped through the little slot.

Annabel sifted through the envelopes, most of them made out to the previous owner or the generic resident. But one hot-pink strawberry-scented envelope was addressed in fancy calligraphy to Ms. Annabel Currin at Fairy Godmother. She stood slowly, a broad smile spreading across her face.

My first official piece of mail.

It suddenly struck her that her dream of opening this shop was becoming a reality.

Annabel wanted to squeal.

There was a sudden knock on the front door and she jumped. She peered through the glass door and then struggled to unlock it. The lock, probably original to the shop, stuck badly because of disuse.

"Mason? What are you doing here? I thought you were going to call when you got back in town."

"I just got back, and I was driving past when I saw your car." He leaned against the door frame and peered at her intently, as if seeing her for the first time.

A gentle breeze stirred the scent of the expensive cologne he preferred. And as always, he looked immaculate in his designer suit and shoes.

"I wish you had called. I don't have your engagement ring. I assume you'd like that back."

"I'm surprised you don't want to hold on to it until the check clears." He laughed bitterly. "I don't have my checkbook with me." He patted the breast pocket of his jacket.

"Then why did you stop?" Annabel folded her arms.

"First, I wanted to tell you how sorry I am. I was an awful boyfriend and an even worse fiancé. But I wanted you to know that I did love you, Annabel. I still do. I never intended to hurt you. And I thought you deserved to hear that in person."

"Thank you, Mason."

Despite the effort Mason had put into looking contrite and sounding sincere, his apology left her completely dissatisfied.

Had he been sincere a single moment in the two years they'd spent together? Looking at him now, she doubted that he ever had.

Suddenly, holding on to the ring until he had reimbursed her in full seemed like a prudent idea.

"You can contact my lawyer, Roarke Perry, to arrange delivery of payment."

"Annabel, wait." He put his hand against the door as she tried to close it. "I wanted to ask if you'll reconsider."

"The amount of the settlement?"

"No. Look, I know what I did was unforgivable, but…I didn't realize how much you meant to me until—"

"Wait, you're not seriously asking to get back together, are you? Because if this is your way of trying to get out of settling my claim—"

"No, I'm being sincere. I'll drop down on one knee again if you want me to," he said.

"You didn't drop down on one knee the first time," she reminded him.

Another sign she'd ignored.

"It's one of the many things I regret about our relationship. I didn't realize until I lost you how important you are to me. I should've supported your dream just as you've supported mine. And if you give me a chance, I swear I'll make it up to you."

"Mason, please, just go away. Pay the claim or don't. But make all further arrangements through my lawyer."

"Annabel!" he called as she shut and locked the door between them. She stood, glaring at him with her arms crossed, until he finally cursed and walked away.

"Why is it that the men in my life only seem fascinated with me once I walk away?" she muttered as she climbed the stairs.

"I can't speak for Mason, but you were right about me. I was terrified of how my feelings for you would change my life." Roarke stepped out into the hall, his hands shoved into the pockets of his gray suit pants.

"You heard that whole thing with Mason?"

He nodded. "I did. As your lawyer, I applaud the way you handled the situation. As the man who has fallen utterly and completely in love with you, I'm incredibly hopeful."

"Did you say—"

"Yes, Annabel." He stepped closer, placing his hands lightly on her hips. "I love you. More than I've ever loved anyone. In a way I didn't even know was possible. You changed everything for me. I never want to go back to the solitary existence I led before I met you. Not without a fight."

Annabel's heart raced and tears stung her eyes. "What about your long list of objections, counselor? Me being fresh out of a relationship? You living in Dallas and me just buying this shop in Houston? What about our fathers hating each other? Are you telling me that none of that matters anymore?"

He cradled her cheek and she leaned into his hand, missing his touch. "I'm saying that you matter so much more. As long as you're by my side, Annabel, together we'll find a way to slay all of those dragons."

Roarke leaned down, and captured her mouth in a kiss, his tongue seeking hers as he held her in his arms.

God, she missed this man.

She missed his subtle humor and sexy smile. His gentle touch and the warmth of his kiss. The perfect way in which their bodies fit together and the passion that ignited between them.

Being with Roarke made her happy. But it was his work in Dallas that made *him* happy. Her bungled, backdoor attempt to persuade him to relinquish the practice made her no better than Mason with his selfish demand that she retire her vlog.

If Roarke gave up the practice he'd been building, just to be with her, wouldn't he eventually resent her for it?

Roarke was surprised when Annabel suddenly pulled away.

"What about your practice in Dallas? I can't ask you to give up something so important to you. And I know you're not interested in a long-distance relationship."

Roarke pressed another kiss to her soft sweet lips. Then he slipped his hand in hers and led her to the sofa in her office, where they both sat down.

"What's that?" He indicated the loud pink envelope in her hand.

A proud smile lit her eyes. "My first official piece of mail." She held it up so that he could see the address. "I can't believe how excited I am over a piece of mail I haven't even read yet."

"Open it."

"Right now? In the middle of our discussion?"

"This is a special moment for Fairy Godmother and for you, Annabel. I want to share it with you."

"Okay." She carefully opened the envelope to preserve it as much as she could. She read the card aloud. It was a thank-you note from a twelve-year-old girl whose mother had been the recipient of one of Annabel's makeovers.

Their family had lost everything after her father's

death from a long painful illness that drained the family's finances. They'd been living in temporary housing and her mother had been struggling to find another job. She'd lost hers while caring for her ill husband. The girl said her mother had found a new job a month after her makeover. Now, three months later, the family was moving into a place of their own.

The family's story was reminiscent of the woman she'd given her very first Fairy Godmother makeover and many of the women in between. She was grateful to have made a difference in those families' lives at a time when they needed it.

"That's amazing." Tears wet Annabel's cheeks. "I'll be able to do this for more women once Fairy Godmother is up and running. I'd even like to expand to helping men, especially struggling vets."

"I'm glad you're doing this, too." His heart swelled with pride. "You're a gift to the world, Annabel. And I don't want to lose you. Even if that means making a change."

She sniffled and wiped away tears. "What kind of change?"

"The false fraud charges against my father helped him see the need to make sure everything is aboveboard, something I've been preaching for a long time. My father is finally ready to listen, for the sake of the company and his legacy. I'm going to be appointed as the Perry Holdings compliance officer or whatever title I think best suits the position."

"Will you be the compliance officer in name only, or will your father allow you to create real change to the company's culture?" Annabel knew enough about Sterling to doubt the sincerity of his offer.

It was a thought that had occurred to him, too. That's why he made his father agree to his terms in writing.

"I'm building our ethics department from scratch. I outlined my terms for taking on this project in writing, and my father has agreed to every one of them. I have complete latitude to implement new policies the way our ethics team sees fit."

"That's fantastic, Roarke. But is that what you really want to do?"

"It is. I've been trying to convince my father to do this for years."

"Is that what made you accept his offer?"

"No. It was something else he said. He said that if I believed things needed to be cleaned up at Perry Holdings, who better to do it than a man with high character and a vested interest in this family's legacy? Then he said that it was the best way to ensure that Perry Holdings is a company I'll be proud to hand over to my children one day."

Annabel squeezed his hand. "And will you be happy?"

He stroked her cheek, a wide grin making his blue eyes twinkle. "Being with you makes me happy, Annabel. Everything else is gravy." He pressed a soft kiss to her lips. "Which brings me to my next question. I've never known anyone like you, Annabel. You are the only woman for me." He kissed her hand. "Will you marry me?"

She stared at him, her head cocked and her eyes blinking rapidly. "Are you serious?"

Roarke got down on one knee and smiled. "I would never have believed in love at first sight if I hadn't met you at Farrah's that day, Lemon Ice. No one in the world is a better match for me than you. I want to spend the rest of my life with you. Will you marry me?"

"Yes, Two Pies." She smiled, tears falling down her cheeks. "Yes, I will."

Epilogue

Angela and Ryder are engaged. Now Annabel and Roarke are, too. But the Perrys and Currins will pay for the devastation they caused my family.

The proposed marriages between the families will build an even stronger alliance between them.

I tried to play by the rules. To work hard and bide my time. But my life keeps spinning out of control while the Perrys and Currins grow wealthier and more powerful.

I lost my beloved father and my child was stolen from me. And Sterling Perry and Ryder Currin and their broods are at the root of it all.

I just wanted them to know a little of my pain. Murder was never part of the plan. But Vincent Hamm left me no choice. Now I'll never be able to scrub the image of his dying expression from my brain or his blood from my hands. But I've come too far. I can't deviate from my plan. Or else poor Vincent will have died in vain.

There'll be no more killing, if it can be helped. But there are fates worse than death a person can suffer.

The Perrys and Currins reign over their gilded kingdoms, flaunting their joyous good fortune. But that won't last for long, starting with Melinda Perry.

Why on earth should she get to be happy and pregnant when her father destroyed my life?

She won't. Not if I have anything to say about it.

* * * * *

*Is Melinda really pregnant? Who wants revenge
on the Perry and Currin families?*

*Find out in the upcoming installments of
Texas Cattleman's Club: Houston*

Read every scintillating episode!

Hot Texas Nights *by USA TODAY
bestselling author Janice Maynard*

Wild Ride Rancher *by USA TODAY
bestselling author Maureen Child*

That Night in Texas *by Joss Wood*

Rancher in Her Bed *by USA TODAY
bestselling author Joanne Rock*

Married in Name Only *by USA TODAY
bestselling author Jules Bennett*

Off Limits Lovers *by Reese Ryan*

Texas-Sized Scandal *by USA TODAY
bestselling author Katherine Garbera*

Tangled with a Texan *by USA TODAY
bestselling author Yvonne Lindsay*

Hot Holiday Rancher *by USA TODAY
bestselling author Catherine Mann*

COMING NEXT MONTH FROM

HARLEQUIN® Desire

Available September 3, 2019

#2683 TEXAS-SIZED SCANDAL
Texas Cattleman's Club: Houston • by Katherine Garbera

Houston philanthropist Melinda Perry always played by the rules. Getting pregnant by a mob boss's son was certainly never in the playbook—until now. Can they contain the fallout...and maybe even turn their forbidden affair into forever?

#2684 STRANDED AND SEDUCED
Boone Brothers of Texas • by Charlene Sands

To keep her distance from ex-fling Risk Boone, April Adams pretends to be engaged. But when a storm strands them together and the rich rancher has an accident resulting in amnesia, he suddenly thinks he's the fiancé! Especially when passion overtakes them...

#2685 BLACK TIE BILLIONAIRE
Blackout Billionaires • by Naima Simone

CEO Gideon Knight demands that Shay Neal be his fake fiancée to avenge his family. Too bad he doesn't realize they already shared an anonymous night during the Chicago blackout! But even through the deception, the truth of their chemistry cannot be denied.

#2686 CALIFORNIA SECRETS
Two Brothers • by Jules Bennett

Ethan Michaels is on a mission to reclaim the resort his mother built. Then he's sidetracked by sexy Harper Williams—only to find out she's his enemy's daughter. All's fair in love and war...until Harper's next explosive secret shakes Ethan to his core.

#2687 A BET WITH BENEFITS
The Eden Empire • by Karen Booth

Entrepreneur Mindy Eden scoffs when her sisters bet she can't spend time with her real estate mogul ex without succumbing to temptation. But it soon becomes crystal clear that second chances are in the cards. Will Mindy risk her business for one more shot at pleasure?

#2688 POWER PLAY
The Serenghetti Brothers • by Anna DePalo

Hockey legend and sports industry tycoon Jordan Serenghetti needs his injury healed—and fast. Too bad he clashes with his physical therapist over a kiss they once shared—and Jordan forgot! As passions flare, will she be ready for more revelations from his player past?

YOU CAN FIND MORE INFORMATION ON UPCOMING HARLEQUIN® TITLES, FREE EXCERPTS AND MORE AT WWW.HARLEQUIN.COM.

HDCNM0819

Get 4 FREE REWARDS!

We'll send you 2 FREE Books plus 2 FREE Mystery Gifts.

Harlequin® Desire books feature heroes who have it all: wealth, status, incredible good looks... everything but the right woman.

FREE Value Over **$20**

SPECIAL EXCERPT FROM

HQN™

For Vanessa Logan, returning home was about healing, not exploring her attraction to cowboy Jacob Dalton! But walking away from their explosive chemistry is proving impossible…

Read on for a sneak preview of
Lone Wolf Cowboy *by* New York Times *and* USA TODAY *bestselling author Maisey Yates.*

She curled her hands into fists, grabbing hold of his T-shirt. And she had no idea what the hell was running through her head as she stood there looking up into those wildly blue eyes, the present moment mingling with memories of that night long ago.

While he witnessed the deepest, darkest thing she'd ever gone through. Something no one else even knew about.

He was the only one who knew.

The only one who knew what had started everything. Olivia didn't understand. Her parents didn't understand. And they had never wanted to understand.

But he knew. He knew and he had already seen what a disaster she was.

There was no facade to protect. No new enlightened sense of who she was. No narrative about her as a lost cause out there roaming the world.

He'd already seen her break apart. For real. Not the Vanessa that existed when she was hiding. Hiding her problems from her family. Hiding her feelings behind a high.

Hiding. And more hiding.

No. He had seen her at her lowest when she hadn't been able to hide.

And somehow, he seemed to bring that out in her. Because she wasn't able to hide her anger.

And she wasn't able to hide this. Whatever the wildness was that was coursing through her veins. No, she couldn't hide that either. And she wasn't sure she cared.

So she was just going to let the wildness carry her forward.

She couldn't remember the last time she had done that. The last time she'd allowed herself this pure kind of over-the-top emotion.

It had been pain. The pain she felt that night she lost the baby. That was the last time she had let it all go. In all the time since then when she had been on the verge of being overwhelmed by emotion she had crushed it completely. Hidden it beneath drugs. Hidden it beneath therapy speak.

She had carefully kept herself in hand since she'd gotten sober. Kept herself under control.

What she hadn't allowed herself to do was feel.

She was feeling now. And she wasn't going to stop it.

She launched herself forward, and her lips connected with his.

And before she knew it, she was kissing Jacob Dalton with all the passion she hadn't known existed inside of her.

Don't miss
Lone Wolf Cowboy *by Maisey Yates,*
available August 2019 wherever
Harlequin® books and ebooks are sold.

www.Harlequin.com

SPECIAL EXCERPT FROM

HARLEQUIN

Desire

CEO Gideon Knight demands that Shay Neal be his fake
fiancée to avenge his family. Too bad he doesn't realize
they already shared an anonymous night during the
Chicago blackout! But even through the deception,
the truth of their chemistry cannot be denied.

Read on for a sneak peek at
Black Tie Billionaire
by USA TODAY bestselling author Naima Simone!

"To answer your other question," he murmured. "Why did I
single you out? Your first guess was correct. Because you are
so beautiful I couldn't help following you around this over-
the-top ballroom filled with people who possess more money
than sense. The women here can't outshine you. They're like
peacocks, spreading their plumage, desperate to be noticed,
and here you are among them, like the moon. Bright, alone,
above it all and eclipsing every one of them. What I don't
understand is how no one else noticed before me. Why every
man in this place isn't standing behind me in a line just for
the chance to be near you."

Silence swelled around them like a bubble, muting the din
of the gala. His words seemed to echo in the cocoon, and he
marveled at them. Hadn't he sworn he didn't do pretty words?
Yet it had been him talking about peacocks and moons.

What was she doing to him?

Even as the question echoed in his mind, her head tilted
back and she stared at him, her lovely eyes darker…hotter. In

that moment, he'd stand under a damn balcony and serenade her if she continued looking at him like that. He curled his fingers into his palm, reminding himself with the pain that he couldn't touch her. Still, the only sound that reached his ears was the quick, soft pants breaking on her pretty lips.

"I—I need to go," she whispered, already shifting back and away from him. "I—" She didn't finish the thought, but turned and waded into the crowd, distancing herself from him.

He didn't follow; she hadn't said no, but she hadn't said yes, either. And though he'd caught the desire in her gaze—his stomach still ached from the gut punch of it—she had to come to him.

Or ask him to come for her.

Rooted where she'd left him, he tracked her movements.

Saw the moment she cleared the mass of people and strode in the direction of the double doors where more tray-bearing staff emerged and exited.

Saw when she paused, palm pressed to one of the panels.

Saw when she glanced over her shoulder in his direction.

Even across the distance of the ballroom, the electric shock of that look whipped through him, sizzled in his veins. Moments later, she disappeared from view. Didn't matter; his feet were already moving in her direction.

That glance, that look. It'd sealed her fate.

Sealed it for both of them.

What will happen when these two find each other alone during the blackout?

Find out in
Black Tie Billionaire
by USA TODAY *bestselling author Naima Simone available September 2019 wherever Harlequin® Desire books and ebooks are sold.*

www.Harlequin.com